Ballet Academy

Find out more about the characters
and the Academy at:

www.balletacademy.co.uk

The *Ballet Academy* series

1) Dance Steps
2) A Question of Character
3) Friends Old and New
4) On Your Toes
5) Dancing in Milan
6) A Tutu Too Many

Companion book:
The World of Ballet

Ballet Academy

On Your Toes

BEATRICE MASINI

Translation by Laura Watkinson

PICCADILLY PRESS • LONDON

First published in Great Britain in 2010
by Piccadilly Press Ltd,
5 Castle Road, London NW1 8PR
www.piccadillypress.co.uk

Text copyright © Beatrice Masini, 2005
English language translation © Laura Watkinson 2010
Translated from the original *Sulle Punte!*
published by Edizioni EL, Trieste, Italy
www.edizioniel.com
Published by arrangement with Rights People, London

A catalogue record for this book is available
from the British Library

ISBN: 978 1 84812 066 2

Printed in the UK by CPI Bookmarque, Croydon, CR0 4TD
Cover design by Patrick Knowles
Cover illustration by Sara Not

Mixed Sources
Product group from well-managed
forests and other controlled sources
www.fsc.org Cert no. TT-COC-002227
© 1996 Forest Stewardship Council
FSC

CHAPTER ONE

A
Present

It was a funny-looking book. It was the shape of a rather chunky ballet shoe, although it really looked more like a clog. The general pinkness, the little bow to tie the book closed and the laced-up ribbons beneath the title created more or less the right impression though. It was called *The Ballerina's Handbook* and you could immediately see that it was meant for very young girls. Zoe's gran had bought it for her as a present. She'd told Zoe she'd spotted it in a bookshop on one of her shopping trips and had thought of Zoe, even though she was obviously a bit too old for it. Her gran had said she knew Zoe was a proper, serious ballerina, not just a little girl fantasising about what she wanted to be when she grew up, but she thought the book was good fun and that it might be a nice addition to Zoe's bookcase.

Zoe had quite a large collection of books about dance, including *Billy Elliot* (the book, but of course she had the film too) and a gorgeous edition of Hans Christian Andersen's fairytale *The Red Shoes*, which was full of illustrations that were pretty, but sad-looking somehow. Then, of course, there were her old Angelina Ballerina books about the little white mouse who dreams of becoming a famous ballerina, the photographic books of little girls in tutus who looked as though they were having loads of fun (Zoe suspected this meant they had no idea what real dancing was all about) and some rather silly stories about girls who had their minds set on just one thing: becoming a prima ballerina – the very best ballerina of all. This was something the Ballet Academy discouraged – it was more important to concentrate on being the best ballerina you could be.

Zoe thought that there was enough room in her collection for the funny shoe-shaped book as well, even though, as she leafed through it, certain phrases that leaped out at her were so odd they almost made her laugh out loud. Such as, *No ballerina can do without a pair of leg warmers*, or, *No ballerina can ever dance without her tutu*, and *A ballerina does not speak to her audience to explain what she wants to say. Instead, she uses her body, her face and her dance steps to explain her emotions.*

As she read the comments, Zoe came up with an idea. She could write her very own handbook for ballerinas. A sort of diary . . . or maybe not. A better idea would be to put together a collection of her own thoughts and reflections. She'd been doing so much thinking lately that she felt as though her head was bursting with a million bustling thoughts. Maybe writing them down would make them easier to understand.

She opened the desk drawer where she kept her blank notebooks. Most of them were the usual boring kind that she used for school, but she had two special ones as well, which were bound like proper little books. One was a birthday present. It was black with red edges and a piece of elastic to keep it closed. The other notebook she'd bought for herself at a wonderful stationery shop. It had a fabric cover with a green checked design and bright blue trimming. The pages inside were completely blank so it would be perfect to use as a diary.

Zoe had never kept a proper diary before. She'd started to write one a while ago for fun but only because her friend Leda was doing it too. Zoe had got bored of it straightaway. It felt silly writing down what had happened to her during the day, because she already knew what she'd done and, besides, it was always the same.

This time she didn't intend to write down things that had happened, but things that she'd thought instead. She took the gold pen that her mum had lent her and started to write. Zoe was only allowed to use the pen at home; her mum had told her not to take it to school in her pencil case because it might get lost. She started by copying the style of the shoe-shaped book, but she soon found her own style.

A ballerina does not speak. She has no need to speak. No, that's not true. Ballerinas actually say a lot, it's just that they don't use words. They have a different vocabulary made up of gestures that express emotions and sensations. The difficult thing is feeling those emotions deeply enough, but if you manage to really feel them, you find that your body follows your mind, and does what it's supposed to, and then you can express anything you want. Well, most of the time, anyway.

The door suddenly flew open, and Maria, her little sister, dashed into Zoe's room with her usual happy lack of respect for Zoe's personal space.

'What are you doing, Zoe?'

'Writing a book,' Zoe said, but Maria's thoughts had already moved on. She ran over to the window, looked outside and said, 'How come you have a nicer view than me? And, come to think of it, your room's bigger than mine as well!'

'But you've got a balcony with all that extra space to play,' Zoe was quick to respond.

When she was smaller she'd been sure that her big sister Sara's room was the best one. *Why should she have all the privileges and advantages just because she's older?* Zoe had thought. Now she'd realised that wasn't always entirely true. Their rooms each had their own advantages. It was true that Zoe's was the biggest and it looked out on to the garden, but you could see for miles from Sara's room when the weather was good, and Maria's room had a balcony to go out on. If only she could only make Maria understand that. In actual fact, Maria understood quite a lot of things, even things you thought she'd missed.

Later that evening, Maria looked at Zoe over the dinner table with a spark of mischief in her eyes. Then she announced, 'Did you know that Zoe's changed her mind about what she wants to be when she grows up?'

'Really?' their dad said, raising his eyebrows.

'Yes. She wants to be a writer now. In fact, she's already started.'

Their mum looked at Zoe. 'Well, that is a big piece of news,' she remarked.

'It's not true,' Zoe insisted, looking daggers at Maria, but it didn't seem to have the slightest effect on her little sister. 'It's just that . . . Oh, nothing. I was just making some notes, that's all.'

Zoe very much hoped that the discussion would finish there. She was rather protective about her own things and her own world. She didn't always feel that way, but she preferred to decide for herself when she was ready to let someone in on something. She'd discovered that about herself recently. She'd always been a little reserved, but now she really felt the need for some privacy.

Her mum and dad seemed to understand this. Dad distracted Maria by asking if she'd done her reading practice.

Maria stared at him, with a look of boredom and irritation on her face, then bowed her head and replied, 'Nooo.'

'We can do it together after dinner,' Sara suggested. Four pairs of eyes turned to stare at her. Girls of fourteen don't normally have much time for their little sisters. Sara certainly didn't usually find any time to spend with Maria. Until now.

'Is that a pig I see flying past?' their mum wondered out loud, peering out of the window.

'Ha ha. Very funny,' Sara said. 'Just because I decide to give my sister a hand for once.'

'A-ha. Yes, you said it. For once,' their dad said. 'So it'll be just this once and that'll be enough for you, I imagine.'

'We'll see,' Sara said, sounding rather annoyed.

Later, they heard snatches of conversation coming from the living room, and various muffled shrieks. Sara obviously didn't have much patience and Maria had clearly had enough and was reading very badly. This might have been because she was tired, or because she wasn't in the mood or the piece she had to read was too difficult. Or perhaps because it was the last bit of free time she had before bed, when your mind needs a little freedom to wander and to do what you feel like doing, rather than what you should be doing. Maria wasn't very good at reading though. It was almost the end of the school year and she was still having problems, so she really needed to practise every day. Zoe felt sorry for her sister, even though she couldn't really relate to how Maria felt – hating printed words and finding them so difficult to decipher. Reading had never been a problem for Zoe. She had learned to read when she was about five, and had discovered that reading was a wonderful key that allowed her to discover the world. She told her mum this when she went to give her a goodnight kiss. Her mum was already tucked up under the covers and leaning back on two pillows with a book in her hands. She sighed and said, 'Children aren't all the same. That's one of the nice things about them. Just think how different the three of you are, even though you're sisters. It's fascinating, but sometimes it can be difficult too.'

'Are you really writing a book?'

Sara had just finished in the bathroom and she was standing in the doorway to Zoe's bedroom with her arms crossed and a curious expression on her face. Zoe looked up from her desk. In the dim light, her big sister was a slim and elegant silhouette. Zoe almost wanted to draw her, but she was totally hopeless at drawing.

'No, of course not,' Zoe said, automatically covering the page with her hand, even though Sara was too far away to read it. 'I'm just putting down a few of my thoughts about dancing.'

'Anita's mum always goes looking for her diary and then reads it in secret. Isn't that dreadful?' said Sara. 'Anita found out because she suspected her mum was up to something, so she slipped a hair into the last page of her diary, and next time she opened the diary, the hair wasn't there. So now she keeps two diaries. There's the original one, which is completely fake. She only writes stuff that's not true in it, you know, harmless things. And she's found a new hiding place for the real diary. Sometimes mums can be your worst enemies,' Sara said.

'Do you keep a diary?' Zoe asked her.

'No. I think it's a waste of time. And you know I don't like writing anyway. I prefer maths.'

'You could invent a secret numerical code and use that to write,' Zoe said. 'Like a spy. That way at least you'd still be using numbers.'

'And go to all that effort? What for? So I can tell a blank page what I've been up to? I don't think so!'

'Usually people keep diaries so that they can work out what they think about things. You write down your thoughts to clear your head,' Zoe said, shrugging her shoulders. 'Well, that's what our English teacher said anyway.'

'Do you know what I do when I need to think things through?' Sara replied. 'I stand in front of the mirror and I talk to myself. Then I repeat what I've said, two or even three times.'

Zoe smiled. 'I do that too.'

'It works, doesn't it?'

'Of course it works.'

'And it wastes a loss less paper too,' said Sara, turning away. 'Less paper, more trees. And I'm on the side of the trees.'

'So am I,' Zoe said with a laugh. 'But if you're worried about the trees, you could always use recycled paper.'

CHAPTER TWO

On
Your Toes

It felt as though all of the girls were going through a major change together: they were finally going *en pointe*! This meant learning to dance on the tips of their toes, and they were doing it ahead of schedule under the watchful gaze of Madame Olenska, head of the Academy, and Gimenez, who was now officially her assistant.

Not very much had happened so far though. They'd had loads of fittings to get the right size shoes. The satin pointe shoes were very glamorous. They were real ballerina's shoes – the sort that you start dreaming about even before you realise you want a pair of your very own. But they were also very fragile – the satin damaged easily and the body of the shoe wore out quickly too. Zoe had heard that some dancers got through a pair of shoes in a single performance, but dance students generally managed to make their shoes last longer than that. After all, it didn't really matter what they looked like when they didn't have an audience.

'My mum said I can have as many new pairs as I like,' Laila announced. 'She says a proper ballerina should always look the part and it doesn't matter how many pairs I get through.'

No one bothered to reply. They were too busy trying to sew ribbons on to their shoes. It was difficult enough pinpointing the right place to put the ribbons on. It all depended on the shape of your foot – if you sewed the ribbons in the wrong place, your shoes wouldn't fit properly. Once you'd worked out where to attach them, you had to sew them on and that was even more of a challenge. Demetra had told them they needed to learn how to do it themselves, without running to their mums all the time or going to the dressmakers, who had a million other things to do. Real ballerinas took care of their own shoes, she said, and she had no intention of sewing on forty ribbons for them. She wasn't their servant – she was a dressmaker. In fact, she was the head dressmaker, thank you very much.

Zoe had never threaded a needle in her life and Demetra, who was watching her hopeless attempts, said,

'Hmm, if I were you, sweetheart, I'd do a bit of practice on an old rag at home before you riddle those poor shoes with holes.'

She was even more abrupt with the others, who she wasn't as close to. 'I think you'd better just give up right now,' she said. But of course no one wanted to admit defeat, so lots of fingers were pricked and drops of blood splashed down on to the floor, just like in a fairytale.

Zoe listened to Demetra's advice and when she got home she asked her mum for a piece of old material and a needle and thread. She fiddled away for a while, making big, messy holes in the cloth until she got fed up and threw it all on the floor. Half an hour later, she picked up the bundle of needle, thread and cloth, tried again, hurt herself, but persevered, puffing and panting, until she finally managed to sew a ribbon to the fabric. It almost looked acceptable. Then she gave it a tug to test how firmly it was fixed. It came away at the third pull. Zoe hurled the whole lot through her bedroom door and on to the landing. Then she went and picked it up, because she didn't want Maria, who tended to walk around with bare feet, to hurt her foot on the needle.

Her mum found her sitting on the bed, with the scrap of material in one hand and a grumpy look on her face. She immediately knew what was wrong – after all, she was the mother of a ballerina. 'Trying to sew your laces on, eh?'

'Yes,' said Zoe, although she didn't want her mum to know that she was feeling disheartened for such a silly reason.

'Aren't you going to show me your pointe shoes?' her mum asked.

Zoe felt a bit stupid, because in all the worry about learning how to sew the laces on, she'd forgotten the shoes were in her bag. She went to fetch them.

'Here they are,' she said, handing them to her mum, who took them from her with a proud smile. Her mum laid the shoes on top of the chest of drawers and slipped one out of its bag. The satin looked pale and shiny, almost luminous. She held up the shoe and turned it over in her hands.

'It looks just like a little boat,' she said, then added, 'What a silly thing to say. It's just that I'm feeling a bit emotional. Aren't you?'

For the first time that day, Zoe wondered if she was indeed feeling emotional. She'd forgotten all about the most important thing: her new pointe shoes. She'd been distracted by all the fuss about having the right size, the ribbons and the disobedient needle . . . But perhaps she was actually distracting herself from her emotions, so that she wasn't overwhelmed. In fact, now that she'd started thinking about the significance of it all, she felt almost paralysed. It was as though her feelings had grabbed her by the throat and wouldn't let go, so much so that she couldn't even answer her mum's question. Her mum put down the shoe next to its twin. Right now there was no difference between the two shoes but their shape would change as Zoe used them.

Her mum hugged Zoe. She was so proud of her little girl, who was growing up in so many ways, and was now learning to stand on the tips of her toes.

'They're beautiful,' she whispered into Zoe's hair.

'Yes,' Zoe managed to say, and then the lump in her throat relaxed and everything went back to normal.

'What about the laces? Do you want me to sort them out for you?'

'Demetra says . . .'

Her mum didn't let her finish. 'Demetra, Demetra, Demetra. I really would like to do it for you, Zoe. The job needs to be done well. You'll have all the time in the world to practise and learn how to do it by yourself. Go on.'

Zoe gave in, thinking how nice it would be if the laces of her first pointe shoes were sewn on by her mum. She had another thought for *The Ballerina's Handbook*:

To become a ballerina, you need a lot of patience. It takes a long time to learn how to do things in the right way, according to the rules.

Madame Olenska was absolutely insistent that the girls should lace up their shoes correctly. 'The ribbons of pointe shoes are made of satin, and they tend to slip,' she said. 'This means it's absolutely essential to do them up correctly. Not too tightly, because that'll hurt your ankles and block your circulation, but not too loose either, because a loose shoe cannot obey your foot. Gimenez, would you show the girls how it's done?'

Gimenez smiled and reached into her black bag. She took out a fabulous pair of red satin shoes that sparkled like jewels and slipped them on. Then she rested one foot on the bench and started lacing up her shoes in slow motion. 'Like thisss . . . and thisss . . . and thisss,' she said, drawing out the *s* with her Spanish accent.

She looks like a painting by Degas, Zoe thought as she watched her. But no, that wasn't quite right. Degas's paintings were all about delicate colours and his ballerinas dressed in white or, at the most, pink, not red and black. It was the way Gimenez was standing that had reminded her of his paintings.

Copying Gimenez was not easy, even after she'd repeated the ceremony of the ribbons a few more times. Nearly all of the girls had tied their laces too loosely – the ribbons slipped down around their ankles the moment they moved. They had to do them all over again, starting at the beginning, and again and again. That was how the whole lesson went – not a single note played, nor one step danced, not a *plié,* not a single *port de bras.* It was very strange indeed.

'That was sooo boring,' Leda said as they were getting changed. 'I'd almost have preferred a whole lesson of barre practice.'

'Well, Madame Olenska really does care about the details,' Zoe said.

'Yes, I know that, but we could practise doing our ribbons at home by ourselves without wasting all that time. Like her over there, for example,' she said, nodding in Laila's direction. Then she lowered her voice. 'She can sort her laces out in a flash. Little Miss Perfect, as always.' She pulled a face at Laila's back, taking advantage of the fact that Laila was picking up her things.

'That's because I prepare properly,' Laila shot back at her, turning round quickly. 'I tried the laces out at home first. And I've been practising dancing *en pointe* too.'

'So you want to go rushing ahead as usual?' Paula joined in from the opposite bench. 'If Madame Olenska says we shouldn't try by ourselves, then we shouldn't – that's all there is to it.'

'Are you going to go and tell her then? Tell tales on me?' Laila scowled.

'I'm not the telltale around here,' Paula snapped. Everyone knew that Laila had tried to get Alissa suspended by telling Gimenez she was too ill to dance.

Laila didn't say a word, but left the changing room pretty quickly.

'Will she ever change?' Anna said with a sigh.

'I don't think so,' Alissa answered. 'But it doesn't matter.'

'Of course it does, she keeps on spoiling everything with her constant need to be the best,' said Anna. 'She's so . . . anxious all the time.'

'That's exactly right, she's anxious. Anxiety's not a nice thing, just let her get on with it. Ultimately, I think she's the one who suffers most,' Alissa said.

Zoe was struck by the wisdom of her words, and she looked at Alissa with a mixture of admiration and surprise.

'So, did you dance *en pointe* today?' Sara asked at dinner.

'Not yet, we had a few problems with the laces,' Zoe said. Then she explained how difficult it was to keep the slippery things in the right place.

'What a pain! You finally arrive at such an important moment and they're still making you wait. It must be driving you crazy.'

'Well, a bit,' Zoe admitted, 'but I suppose this is all about discipline too, in a way.'

'Discipline. What an ugly word!' Sara said. 'It makes me think of those schools in the old days where they used to whack children with a cane.'

'Whack them? On the bum?' asked Maria, with great interest.

'No, usually on the hand, or sometimes on the legs. It must have really hurt.'

'What a mean thing to do,' Maria said.

'Discipline isn't always a bad thing. It means accepting the rules because you understand that they're important,' their dad interrupted.

'Yes, I understand that, but what about passion and enthusiasm? Zoe's dying to get up on to the tips of her toes and dance,' Sara said. 'It's cruel to make her wait so long, isn't it?' She turned to look at Zoe.

Zoe thought for a moment. 'I don't know. I definitely want to do it. But it's so close now that I'm almost enjoying the wait. It's like a really nice chocolate, you know? You don't want it to be gone, so you delay the moment of pleasure. You look at it, you smell it, you hold it in your hand . . .'

'Ooh, is there any chocolate left over from the Easter eggs?' Maria said, and everyone burst out laughing. 'Let's eat it!'

It turned out there was quite a bit of chocolate left, all wrapped up in silver foil. Together they ate up the big chunks of milk and plain chocolate; Maria's suggestion had been a very good one.

All too soon it was time for their first attempt at dancing *en pointe*. Cautiously, they hoisted themselves up on to the unfamiliar supports – the small platform of layered fabric and glue in the tips of their pointe shoes. Their feet felt heavy, and uncertain. Resting the weight of an entire body on such a small area seemed quite risky. Fortunately, their beloved barre was there to offer support, and the exercises slowly became less clumsy, if not exactly confident. It was all about trying to stand naturally on the tips of your toes and using the weight of your body to force the new shoe to follow the curves of your foot. The satin got dirty straightaway; all you had to do was accidentally brush one foot over the over and the satin started to fray and the pink turned grey. If you tried to rub the marks off, it just made things worse.

'What a mess,' Leda complained afterwards in the changing room. 'They're already fit for the bin.'

'Oh, don't exaggerate,' Francine said to her, studying her own shoes with all the attention of a butterfly spotter who's just seen a very rare species. 'I like them like this. You know, a bit "lived in". When Mariah Simone's practising, she always wears shoes that are a bit bashed about. Haven't you ever noticed?'

'Of course, but she's got feet of steel. She could probably manage to dance *en pointe* even without shoes,' Estella replied.

'Maybe it's all about superstition,' Zoe said, thoughtfully.

'Superstition? What do you mean?' Sophie asked.

'Like a magic charm. If you wear old shoes, the new show will be a success. That kind of thing.'

'You're strange,' Sophie said to Zoe, giving her a puzzled

look. 'Where do you get such weird ideas from?'

'Don't you have a lucky charm or a mascot?' Zoe replied.

'Of course I do,' Sophie said.

'And is it old and worn or is it brand new?'

'It's an old thing. But I'm not telling you what it is, because it's a secret.'

'I don't need to know what it is, but don't you see that you have your own superstitions too?'

Sophie just looked at her. She didn't seem to get it at all. The others were all nodding though, and Zoe saw a flash of understanding pass over each of their faces.

When Zoe met Roberto at the foot of the stairs that afternoon, he seemed ecstatic. He took her hand and made her do a pirouette.

'What's happened?' she asked him. 'Have you won a scholarship to the Bolshoi or something?'

'No, it's just that Kai's such a great teacher. He's asked us to design our own choreography. The piece of music's the same for everyone – Ravel – but we can do whatever we like. He wants to see what we've come up with in ten days' time, so I'm off to buy the CD and then I'll get down to work. It's fantastic, you lot going *en pointe* and us boys having extra lessons in character dance. Absolutely brilliant.'

Zoe felt a tiny twinge of envy – she really loved Kai's

lessons too – but it vanished instantly. She was happy for Roberto, because he wanted to be a choreographer when he grew up and this would be a chance for him to put his skills to the test.

After school, they went together to the CD shop. Roberto headed straight for the classical music department, but Zoe stopped at the pop section. Her eyes were drawn to a cover with lots of cows on. It was at number three in the charts that week and the shop had listening posts so that you could listen to the popular CDs. Zoe slipped on the headphones and found herself isolated, in a world of new sounds, listening to the strange words of this unfamiliar song. It didn't really seem to have anything at all to do with cows. The words flowed freely over the music, and the singer had a clear voice. He was singing about success, about climbing up and then falling back down again, that kind of thing. Then, without really thinking about it, Zoe slipped off the headphones, picked up the CD, headed for the cash desk, and paid for it. She looked around as she waited for Roberto. A boy with dreadlocks had picked up the headphones she'd been using and was bobbing his mop of hair around to the beat of the music. Zoe had heard that you shouldn't wash dreadlocks. She washed her hair every other day, and every day in the summer, and she couldn't stand the thought of unwashed hair. *It'd be really difficult to put dreadlocks up in a neat bun, anyway,* she mused. She smiled to herself at the silly thought and looked around at all the other people, of all ages, who were making funny faces as they listened in private to their music. In the background, an irritating tune was thudding away, but it was obvious that everyone had come to the shop to find their own song and you could tell from most people's expressions if they'd found what they were looking for. Some of them looked as though they could spend all day there, listening to their song over and over again.

As she settled down in bed, Zoe put her earphones in, so she wouldn't disturb anyone, and pressed play on the CD player. She'd always liked the rainbow flashes of the CD as it started up and whizzed round, but was a bit frustrated that she didn't understand how it worked. Perhaps it was nicer that way, though, if it remained a mystery. She had another listen to the cow song that wasn't about cows and looked for the words of the chorus in the booklet. All of the words were perfectly clear now that she could read them and listen to them at the same time.

Up and up you go
Higher and higher
Then you slide back down
Don't lose your inner fire
Success is out there

It's no easy prey
Catch it? Let it go?
It's up to you to say . . .

Now that she could see the words written down on paper, they seemed ordinary somehow, less poetic, but the meaning was all that really mattered. The words made a lot of sense to Zoe; they said something about the way she was feeling. She felt as though she was climbing higher and higher to reach important goals. That meant you had to run risks, challenge yourself and understand what really counted. Even something that should come naturally to a ballerina, like learning to dance on the tips of your toes, almost felt like a competition in itself. Would you win? Would it be difficult? Would it be possible? Of course it would. Every girl who wants to become a ballerina has to learn how to dance *en pointe*. But maybe that was when you discovered whether it was really what you wanted to do, whether you really had that talent, that ability. If dancing was your gift and your path in life. What if it all went wrong? What if that was the moment when you slid back down?

Catch it? Let it go? It's up to you to say.

What if Zoe suddenly found out that dance wasn't for her? What might she want to do instead? Was there something she'd like to do more than anything else?

No, not at the moment. That was the only answer

she could come up with, but she was tired and only just managed to take the earphones out before she fell asleep. Otherwise the music might have worked its way inside her head and given her strange, strange dreams.

CHAPTER THREE

A Revelation

'Shall we go home together today?' Alissa asked Zoe.

Zoe quickly thought about it: Roberto was staying after school to work on his choreography and Leda's dad was picking her up that night, so it was fine. 'Okay,' she said. 'Meet you at the entrance later.'

Zoe and Alissa had seen quite a lot of each other lately, but only casually, without making any real effort to spend time together. They'd done a geography project together – something really dull about the Earth's different climatic zones. They'd made it easier by dividing up the work, and had got a good grade for it in the end. Leda had said, 'I'll put up with you and Alissa working together, just this once!' but she'd only meant it as a joke. She'd done her project on the greenhouse effect with Lucas and they'd just about scraped an okay mark, but they seemed quite happy with it.

After school, Zoe went back to the classroom to fetch a book she'd forgotten, and it occurred to her that Alissa might have something she wanted to say to her. When Zoe saw Alissa coming down the stairs and walking towards her, she knew that her suspicions were right. Alissa looked very serious indeed. Her big eyes seemed a shade darker than usual, and a slight crease had appeared between her eyebrows. She was smiling, but you could tell that it was an effort.

They walked to the bus stop, side by side, talking about this and that – grades, the test the next day, homework for Tuesday and the bright red varnish that had appeared on Gimenez's fingernails (from up close, you could see that she had a tiny ladybird with black dots in the centre of each nail).

The bus was late and Alissa was obviously getting impatient. Zoe was sure that it wasn't because of the wait, so she decided to ask her straight out. She looked Alissa in the eye. 'So, what is it you want to say to me?'

Alissa blushed. 'Is it that obvious?'

'Pretty much,' Zoe said, smiling at her friend. 'You've been on tenterhooks for quarter of an hour. Tell me –

you'll feel better afterwards.'

'You're right,' Alissa said. She took a deep breath, but then the bus came round the corner. The girls climbed on and found two seats, one behind the other. Once the noise of the doors shutting had stopped, Alissa turned to look at Zoe and said, 'Do you remember when I told you there was someone I liked and I was trying to make him notice me?'

'Of course,' said Zoe, who remembered it very well.

'Well . . . that someone was . . . Roberto.'

Zoe noticed that Alissa was blushing again, a pinkish glow flushing up her neck to her cheeks.

'But that was absolutely ages ago,' Zoe said. 'You never mentioned it again and I thought . . .'

'You thought I'd got over it? Me too. But when I got back to school after I was ill, I realised that I felt just the same as before. Only I didn't know that you and Roberto were together. You're so . . .'

'Discreet?' Zoe suggested.

'Yes, that's it, discreet. I mean, you're not hugging all the time, you're not always on your own, just the two of you, and no one said anything to me about it, so I thought he was still . . . available. But then I got it. I mean, now I understand. I just wanted to tell you, you know, it's fine now, but . . . you're my friend, and he's my friend, and you're both so nice and kind, and you make a really good couple. I felt a bit upset about it all at first, but then I thought about it and, well, you know, it's fine. Really. I liked Roberto, and I still like him, of course, but not in that way. I like him as a friend. And I like you as a friend. So I wanted to clear the air, just in case you had any doubts . . .'

Alissa stopped to swallow. She was obviously finding it hard to confess her secret. Zoe raised one hand to tell her to stop. 'Okay, it's fine. You've said enough. I get it.'

Alissa laughed with relief. 'It's just that it was a difficult thing to say and it was, you know, a bit awkward and —'

'Are you off again?'

Alissa gave another laugh. 'No, I promise.' Then she looked serious. 'Look, I like spending time with you. With all of you, I mean. Leda too, and Lucas. You're all so nice.'

'You've already said that, but it's not true,' said Zoe.

Alissa gave her a slightly puzzled look.

'What I mean,' Zoe continued, 'is that we're not just spending time with you to be nice. It's because we like you too, that's all.'

'It's important to me,' Alissa said. 'Everyone at home still treats me as though I'm ill. No . . . more like someone who's recovered but could have a relapse at any moment. They're watching me all the time, keeping me under observation. Thank goodness you lot don't do the same. I couldn't bear it.'

'But do you understand why you were ill?' Zoe had wanted to ask her that question for so long. Now seemed like the right moment. She waited for Alissa to answer.

'I think so,' Alissa said. 'I expected too much of myself, and not in a good way. I wanted to be the perfect ballerina and I started to think that being a very thin ballerina was the easiest way to be perfect. So I ate less food. Stupid, eh?'

'No, you're not stupid,' Zoe said to her. 'Hey, it's your stop.'

Alissa shot to her feet, dashed to the open doors of the bus and leaped off. Then she waved at Zoe until the doors closed and she disappeared.

Of course Alissa wasn't stupid. She had just been under a lot of pressure. *Can I cope with the pressure?* Zoe wondered, with a little concern. *Maybe all it would take is just a small thing – a difficulty, a disappointment – and I'd end up with thousands of problems pressing down on me too. Or maybe just one problem, but a gigantic one. Let's hope not,* she concluded, and she automatically crossed the fingers of her right hand, which was tucked away in her pocket.

Of course, she had known that Alissa liked Roberto, but it really had been ages ago. It had been during that time when all of her friends had felt the need to say that they fancied *someone*, maybe even two or three boys at once. She hadn't even given it a thought. Things had worked out by themselves and it was better that way. *It would be terrible if Leda and I liked the same boy,* Zoe thought. *Which would be stronger? Our friendship or the way we felt about him? And what if we had to choose? Let's hope it never happens.*

A row of little, stunted trees ran between the bus stop and Zoe's home. They seemed to be having difficulty growing, but they'd covered themselves in little pink flowers to compensate. The petals were so fragile that all it took was the slightest breath of wind to tear them from the trees. They covered the pavement like a pink carpet and little clouds swirled around Zoe's shoes with every step she took.

What a waste, she thought. *The flowers look lovely on the trees. Spring can be so cruel.*

At that moment, her mobile vibrated in her pocket. It was a text message from Roberto. *Just finished. V tired. Thinking of you.*

Spring can be so sweet too.

CHAPTER FOUR

Arabesques and Embroidery

'Madame Olenska says not to put on your pointe shoes today. Wear your ballet slippers instead,' Gimenez announced from the door of the changing room.

The girls continued to stare at the doorway, even after she'd disappeared in a flash of red and black, the white of her dazzling smile surrounded by the reddest lipstick in the world.

'Ohhh,' Francine grumbled. 'Just when I was starting to get used to them.'

'Used to them? We haven't even started getting blisters. I haven't seen any blood yet either,' Stephanie said, almost seeming to relish the thought.

'Some people never bleed at all. It's all a question of ability really,' said Laila, butting in. Obviously she was referring to herself. Not a single person turned to look at her.

Putting soft ballet slippers back on again was torture for everyone. They felt so saggy and baggy and grey and dull after the brilliant sparkle of the pointe shoes. It was all in their minds, but their feet felt so much heavier. They were like a herd of elephants as they trudged to the lesson.

'I would like to concentrate on arabesques today,' Madame Olenska announced when they had all taken up their positions at the barre. The boys were there too, looking a little annoyed (or at least that's how Lucas and Roberto looked) because it meant that they had to miss out on their extra character dance lesson.

Arabesques were a tricky business. There are few steps and few positions that conceal so many traps – everything is the opposite of what it seems. When it's done well, an arabesque is a marvel of nature that challenges both physics and equilibrium. You lift your leg high up behind you and tilt your body gently forward. Then you hold the position, perfectly immobile. No trembling, no hesitation: a smile on your lips, as if it were normal standing there like that, suspended between heaven and earth.

Without a doubt, Laila was the best at arabesques. They took it in turns to do the exercise so that Madame Olenska could check every single muscle and the others could watch as you did your arabesque, because that was a good learning opportunity too. As Zoe watched Laila, she couldn't help but think of a loose-limbed doll, like a Barbie, who you can do what you want with, changing the angles of the legs and the knees as you like, putting them in completely ridiculous positions. It looked as though a huge, invisible hand was moving Laila's legs from one position to another (if she listened carefully, Zoe imagined she might hear the sound of plastic on plastic, *click, click, click*) and holding her in those impossible postures. Her torso and her leg formed a wide, tilted, perfect V. There was no uncertainty to Laila's movements. She was an arabesque machine. 'Good,' murmured Madame Olenska, without even touching her or correcting anything.

When it was her turn, Zoe tried her very hardest. She wanted to look at herself in the mirror, but that wasn't allowed so she concentrated on her muscles, which screamed as she stretched them out, and she focused on keeping her balance.

'Good,' said Gimenez, and Madame Olenska just nodded. Zoe couldn't see her clearly. She wasn't supposed to take her eyes from the fixed point in front of her, so she just saw an outline moving on the edge of her field of vision, but Madame's silent approval was enough. It made her feel as though the arabesque could last for an eternity and that nothing could distract or bother her. In that moment of absolute, total certainty, Zoe felt tall and strong and able to do anything she wanted. Was it really possible that performing an exercise successfully could make you feel this way? Yes, it was. It really was. When Madame walked past her and stopped by Francine, and Gimenez tapped Zoe's arm to tell her she could relax, she spent another moment enjoying the perfection, appreciating her own hard work.

'Aren't they beautiful? Mum says they're going to be *the* shoes to wear this summer. If you don't have a pair, you're nobody.' As usual, Leda had something Zoe didn't, but she showed them off with such enthusiasm that it didn't annoy Zoe.

Zoe, sitting beside Leda on her bed with its bright-pink quilt, dedicated herself for a few seconds to the careful study of the shoes in question: yes, she had to confess, they were indeed absolutely beautiful. They were made of shiny, ruby red fabric, perhaps satin or silk, with two rows of beads running all the way around the edge and tiny clusters of other beads and embroidery sprinkled here and there on the material, like flowers in a meadow. A thread of gold decorated the shoes in precise and complicated swirls and whirls. They were like arabesques of a different kind. She was seeing arabesques everywhere now.

'They look like slippers to me,' Zoe said. They were soft with rounded toes and were open at the back, and, as far as Zoe was concerned, that made them slippers.

'Slippers? Slippers?!' Leda's reaction was exaggerated, but she was just playing around. 'Don't you think they're rather glamorous for slippers, sweetie? Unless you mean Cinderella-type slippers, of course. Come on, admit it. They're absolutely beautiful, aren't they? Bet you'd like a pair too, wouldn't you? If you're a good girl, I'll ask Mum where she bought them and I might just get some for you,' Leda said to her.

'And what do I have to do to be a good girl?' Zoe asked, playfully.

'Oh, I don't know. How about organising one of our days out? Just the four of us. This time, let's leave Alissa out of it, shall we? Five's a silly number to go out with. There's always one person too many.'

'You're usually the official organiser,' Zoe said, studying her friend. Leda seemed oddly embarrassed. She changed position, and curled up, hugging her knees and resting her head on them. Finally, she said, 'Yes, I know. But I don't feel like it.'

'Aren't you feeling well?'

'No, that's not what I meant. It's just that . . . I don't

want to phone Lucas. He makes me feel . . . awkward.'

Zoe was confused. If she knew one person who was incapable of making anyone feel awkward, it was Lucas. She frowned, paused for a second, then raised her eyebrows. With a gentle smile of realisation, she said, 'Don't tell me you're in love with Lucas!'

Leda blushed and threw a lace cushion at Zoe, which Zoe easily dodged, and then said, 'Well, not exactly. Let's just say I've started to see him in a new light. You know, it's strange . . .' Her expression became more serious, so Zoe listened carefully to what Leda was telling her. 'I never really noticed him before. I mean, I looked at him, but I didn't really see him. I don't know . . . It was as if he was just part of the landscape or something like that. Then one day I found myself looking at his hands. Have you ever noticed how gorgeous his hands are?'

Lucas was one of Zoe's best friends, but at that moment she honestly could not recall his apparently amazing hands.

'And his wrists? He has such strong wrists . . . And such smooth skin.'

Smooth skin, Zoe thought. *Who notices that kind of thing?* But she didn't say anything to Leda. If, as her friend claimed, she wasn't exactly in love with Lucas, then she was something very, very close to it.

They had dinner together, with Leda's mum, who was quite happy to reveal the name of the secret place where you could buy the slippers. She served up a delicious pizza, which she'd ordered in from a new pizza place. Leda's pizza was covered with tuna and peppers and Zoe chose a more modest Margherita. For dessert, there was classic chocolate and vanilla ice cream, with a delicious dusting of chopped nuts on top.

Zoe stayed over that night. They had sleepovers every now and then and Zoe generally preferred to stay over at Leda's rather than the other way round, because Zoe's house was pretty crowded already. Leda's place was so calm and quiet and orderly.

Before they went to sleep, they usually chatted for a long time, but not that night, even though Zoe could see in the gentle glow of Leda's nightlight (Leda said she still couldn't sleep without it) that her friend hadn't closed her eyes. She reached out from the spare bed and took Leda's hand, without saying a word. Leda just squeezed Zoe's hand in response. Her best girl friend fancied her best boy friend. Whatever would happen next?

For a while, nothing happened. They didn't manage to organise an outing until the following Saturday because they had such a lot of homework and tests to do that it would have been difficult to squeeze in a mid-week visit to the cinema. Leda spent much of the eternal wait tormenting Zoe with her mood swings. One moment she was going all gooey about one of the many virtues that she'd suddenly recognised in Lucas and the next moment she was paralysed with anxiety: 'Are you certain he likes me? You know, at least as a friend? Has he ever said anything nice about me to you? He's never told you he fancies anyone else, has he?' It was a barrage of questions and Zoe had soon had enough. She didn't know what to say to Leda, partly because there was no real answer to a lot of her questions. Zoe was fond of Lucas, and didn't want to put words in his mouth. It was a complicated balance. It felt as though it was all about arabesques again, but mental ones this time.

She was tempted to say to Leda, *Just leave me out of it. This concerns you and only you. It's nothing to do with me. I can't help you.* Then she decided to go for the simplest option, which was to listen without making any comments, because she realised that what Leda really needed was someone to listen to her. Then whatever was going to happen would just happen.

On the afternoon of the much-discussed day out, they were walking through the park to get to the city centre when the most violent storm that Zoe could remember suddenly exploded above their heads. The rain was so heavy and unexpected that the four of them split up into pairs. They were separated by sheets of grey water and couldn't even see each other. Roberto took Zoe's hand

and they dashed to shelter in a kind of gazebo, together with a mother and two small children. The children were anxious and impatient and they wanted to leave. Their mother didn't know how to calm them down, so in the end Zoe and Roberto started playing with them to distract them. The storm lasted a really long time. Every now and then it showed signs of stopping, but then it started up again, even stronger than before. The claps of thunder were a bit scary out there in the open, but luckily the children didn't notice because Roberto was acting out all of the animals in Noah's ark for them, from the first in line to the very last, and they were absolutely fascinated – he was a trained dancer after all. Their mother was captivated too, and the children wanted an encore performance, even when it had stopped raining. By the time Roberto had worked through his repertoire for the second time, the sun had come out. The mother and children walked off, turning round to wave again and again. Then Zoe finally got to ask the question that had been bothering her. 'Where have Leda and Lucas got to?'

She didn't find out until later that evening, because they didn't get any answers to the text messages they sent from their phones, and neither of them actually felt brave enough to call and ask. Zoe and Roberto just stayed there in the dripping-wet gazebo, saying sweet things to each other and then sitting together in silence, watching as the sun tried to dry the world. It was so much fresher and brighter after the unexpected shower. The afternoon had certainly not been a failure. In fact, Zoe was relieved to have avoided having to watch Leda's attempts to charm Lucas. Once Leda got an idea into her head, she was unbearable until she'd got what she wanted.

The phone finally rang that evening when Zoe was at home. Her dad answered and called her. 'It's Leda for you. Are you going to take it here or in the hallway?'

A moment later, Zoe was sitting cross-legged, leaning against the wall, winding the telephone cord around her finger (the cordless was more handy, it was true, but this one was much nicer to use) and listening to Leda's story. It was like watching a trailer: being presented with just a few clips in no particular order, with a few words to link them together, but they're not really intended to explain anything, just to create a sense of mystery, to make you want to go and see the film. Leda kept flashing backwards and forwards in time too, but Zoe managed to deduce a few facts:

1. Leda's shoes were ruined because of course she was wearing them, but they weren't waterproof.

2. Lucas had been an 'absolute sweetheart' (actual quote).

3. Life was wonderful.

4. Life was complicated.

5. You never know what's going to happen.

'Don't be in too much of a hurry,' she said to Leda. She had to laugh when she thought about it later. Of course Leda was in a hurry. She was used to getting whatever she wanted immediately. Perhaps because she was an only child, or perhaps because she was just made that way. Maybe it was a combination of the two. With relationships, though, both of you had to want the same thing, and that was where it all started to get complicated.

At the end of the phone call, Zoe realised that she really wanted to hear Lucas's version, to know what had really happened. At least she would hear his point of view, although she realised that still wouldn't be the actual truth. She was curious, but there's a fine line between curiosity and nosiness, and she wasn't sure that she wanted to cross that line. So she left the telephone and went off to bed rather amused, a little bit worried for Leda (although not too much), but mainly happy because she had had such a wonderful, and inspiring afternoon.

A thought for *The Ballerina's Handbook*:

Arabesques are so complicated, yet simple. In a way, they symbolise the life of a ballerina: doing complicated things, but making them look simple. And that's no easy task.

CHAPTER FIVE

Communication

Alice: 'Right now, I'm looking out at the sea. The sun's going down. The sky's all red, with a strip of blue up high and a band of pink on the horizon. It really does look very romantic.'

Zoe (twiddling the phone cord): 'I imagine you've had enough of all that romance, seeing as you get to see the sun going down over the ocean three hundred and sixty five days a year.'

Alice: 'Three hundred and thirty five, if you don't mind. I do go away on holiday sometimes – it's where I met you, remember? Speaking of which, have your family decided whether you're going back to the same place in the mountains this year?'

Zoe: 'Yes, Mum's just confirmed the booking.'

Alice: 'Fantastic.'

Zoe: 'She didn't have any choice. When she suggested going to a different place, she had a revolution on her hands.'

Alice: 'Where did she want to take you?'

Zoe: 'Some farmhouse in the back of beyond. Sara said she'd go on hunger strike. Maria just started screaming.'

Alice: 'If I know you, you kept quiet and let them get on with it.'

Zoe: 'There was enough noise already, I can tell you. Anyway, it was pretty clear how things were going to turn out.'

Alice: 'Don't worry. If it had all gone wrong, I'd have come and kidnapped you. Seriously though, you could always have come and stayed with us for a while.'

Zoe: 'But it's better this way.'

Alice: 'Yeah, and it means I won't have to put up with you at night. What about Roberto then?'

Zoe: 'What about him?'

Alice: 'Is he coming on holiday with you?'

Zoe: 'You are joking, I hope.'

Alice: 'Of course I'm joking. If you bring your boyfriend on holiday, it's not going to be much fun for me, is it?'

Zoe: 'Don't call him my boyfriend.'

Alice: 'Why? What is he?'

Zoe: 'Erm . . .'

Alice: 'Lost your tongue, eh?'

Zoe: 'Can we change the subject?'

Alice: 'Shall we talk about the weather?'

Zoe: 'No. Let's talk about your boyfriends instead.'

Alice: 'Nothing to declare. But that's fine. I'm really busy with schoolwork and stuff and I don't really have time for anything else at the moment.'

Zoe: 'But just a few weeks ago you told me about that friend of your brother's . . .'

Alice: 'Sorry. There must be a problem with the line. All I can hear is crackling . . .'

Zoe (laughing): 'Yeah, right. Okay then, if you want to be all mysterious about it . . .'

Alice: 'He's coming on holiday with us. Well, with my brother.'

Zoe: 'Great. So I'll get to meet him.'

Alice: 'Calm down. I don't know, you ballerinas, you look all delicate and fragile . . .'

Zoe: 'And?'

Alice: 'Well, you only look delicate and fragile. In actual fact, you're like an unstoppable tank.'

Zoe: 'Oh, yes, that's me all right. So why does everything feel so difficult sometimes? I'm never sure that I'm doing the right thing.'

Alice: 'Yeah, I know all about that. You don't need to tell me.'

Background voice: 'Will you get off the phone now, Alice? I need to make a call for work.'

Alice (in a hurry): 'Sorry, it's Mum. She wants me to hang up. Talk later. Byeee.'

Zoe: 'Bye, Alice.'

Roz: 'Hello, this is Roz. Could I speak to Zoe, please?'

Zoe: 'Hi Roz. It's me.'

Roz: 'What? Has your voice changed, the way it does with boys?'

Zoe: 'Ha ha. It's really nice to hear from you too!'

Roz: 'Well, if I were waiting for you to call me . . .'

Zoe: 'What? It's not a competition to see who calls first, is it?'

Roz: 'Yeah, you're right. I was just calling to ask if you wanted to come to my music recital. It should be at the end of the year, but we're doing it a bit early because some people have exams coming up and they need to study. It'll be fun. It's not the usual torture, with all the little kids. There won't be anyone under ten, just the older students.'

Zoe: 'Great. When is it?'

Roz: 'Thursday evening, in exactly a week. We'll come and pick you up if you like. If you want to bring someone else, just let me know so we can reserve the seats. But you'll have to tell me this evening, okay?'

Zoe: 'Okay, thanks. I'll text you.'

Roz: 'Fine. Bye.'

Zoe: 'Hi.'

Roberto: 'Hi. This feels pretty strange, talking to you in the evening.'

Zoe: 'It's an emergency.'

Roberto: 'What's happened?'

Zoe: 'Oh no, nothing bad. It's just that I wanted . . . I was wondering . . . erm, would you like to come to a music recital with me next week?'

Roberto: 'Who's playing?'

Zoe: 'Roz. A friend of mine. She plays the saxophone.'

Roberto: 'A girl who plays the sax? Great. How are you getting there?'

Zoe: 'In the car with Roz and her family.'

Roberto: 'Hang on a sec and I'll go and ask Mum.' [A moment later.] 'She says it's fine.'

Zoe: 'Great. It's going to be fun. Roz is really nice.'

Roberto: 'Yes, but she'll be really nervous, won't she? And we'll have to come straight home afterwards. Or were you thinking of going out clubbing?'

Zoe: 'Ha ha, stupid.'

Roberto: 'You know, I like it when you call me stupid.'

Zoe: 'You sound even more stupid when you say that kind of thing.'

Roberto: 'I know.'

Zoe (laughing): 'Well, that's okay then.'

Roberto (serious): 'Goodnight, Zoe.'

Zoe (serious): 'Goodnight, Roberto.'

Zoe sent the text message she'd promised Roz, then stretched out on the bed with her mobile lying on her tummy like a little cat. It even purred when Roz answered her text. Then she turned off her mobile, because she wouldn't need it again that evening, and thought about how she didn't really like talking on the phone. She preferred emails or text messages. Best of all, she liked looking at the people she was talking to, seeing their expressions, understanding what they were thinking about. She thought she might like to receive a love letter, the way girls did in the old days, but it wasn't exactly something you could ask for, was it? Then there was the fact that Roberto still had a few problems with written English and he'd be bound to make some mistakes if he wrote her a love letter. It might make her laugh and then all the magic would be gone. Or perhaps not.

'Are you okay, Mousie?' Her mum came in to say goodnight. She sat on the edge of Zoe's bed and gave her hair a ruffle.

'You haven't called me Mousie for ages,' said Zoe.

'You're right,' her mum said. 'It just slipped out. Usually I manage to stop myself. I thought you might not like it anymore. You're growing up and I can't keep on treating you like my little baby girl. Even though, to me, you'll always be my little baby girl.'

As she spoke to Zoe, her mum looked at her and even in the dim light of the bedroom, Zoe could see her expression. It was a look of affection, mixed with mid-week tiredness. *I like her like that,* Zoe thought. And then she wondered: *What does my face say? Maybe nothing at all. Maybe there's no emotion there, like a puppet that always has the same look on its face. Perhaps I look as fake as Laila when she smiles while she's doing the most beautiful arabesques in the world . . .*

She wanted to know. 'Mum, can you tell what I'm thinking? By looking at my face, I mean.'

Her mum was a bit confused. She thought about it. 'Now or in general?'

'In general.'

'Yes, I think so. Some people are very good at hiding what they're feeling. It's as though they're wearing a mask all the time. I think it's a way of protecting themselves from their emotions. And there are other people who are completely transparent. You, my dear, are pretty much transparent. Right now, for example, I can read on your face that you're tired, that you're curious, that you've got all these thoughts in your head, that you love me, that you're happy that I'm here . . . Or am I wrong?'

'No, no. You've read almost everything,' Zoe said.

'So what have I missed?' her mum asked, curiously.

'Just one thing. That I like it when you call me Mousie.'

CHAPTER SIX

Silence

Leda was not talking. And what she wasn't talking about was Lucas, of course. Zoe wasn't naturally nosy so she didn't ask any questions. Leda's face said it all, anyway. Her eyes were fixed on the back of Lucas's head, on the back of his neck, on his shoulders. His desk was in the second row and Leda and Zoe sat right at the back of the class, but Leda still didn't miss out on the slightest movement, the quiver of a muscle, the twitch of his elbows within his sweatshirt or his fingers as they rubbed the back of his neck. That had been one of Lucas's little tics ever since Zoe had known him, which had been practically forever. She wondered how he managed to remain so relaxed, how he couldn't feel Leda's stare drilling into him, trying to steal all of his secrets . . . A back couldn't really have that many secrets, she supposed, as she wondered what Leda was feeling and what she hoped to gain by staring at him like that. She could only imagine that it made Leda feel happy, that she liked being in love and that this was all part of the game, maybe even the best part. Zoe couldn't help but think of the whole thing as something like the country dances that Kai made them do, where the dancers laced coloured ribbons around a tall pole and pretended to be country boys and girls flirting with each other.

One of the other classes had performed a country dance called *Midsummer* in the previous year's recital. Zoe remembered it very well. The girls all looked beautiful in their high-waisted dresses and bonnets, as they swirled around and took hold of the boys, who were dressed in simple, black leggings and white open-necked shirts. By the end, they were all whirling around the pole like mad things. Lucy had been wearing the most beautiful costume. It was bright yellow with a striped band around the waist. She looked like a little piece of sunshine. She'd let Zoe try on her bonnet in the dressing room and her reflection in the mirror looked so different, so old-fashioned, with her hair covered and her face poking out.

But she was wandering away from the point, as usual.

Thoughts were so unpredictable. You started by thinking about one thing and, before you knew it, you were thinking about something else entirely. That was the nice thing about daydreaming. You never knew where you were going to end up.

Leda wasn't saying much and whatever she did say revealed that she had only one subject on her mind.

'I watched *Romeo + Juliet* on DVD again yesterday evening. You know, Claire Danes isn't actually beautiful as such. She's got a bit of an odd face. It's too round. But she's such a good actress. And he's fantastic. Leonardo DiCaprio, I mean, but then everyone knows that.'

Or: 'Take a look at this.' Leda pushed her diary towards Zoe, open to a page from a couple of months ago. It was free from lists of homework or lessons – instead Leda had copied out a love poem in purple ink in unusually tidy handwriting.

'Isn't it lovely?'

'Yeah. Who's it by?' Zoe asked.

'What? Didn't I make a note of the poet's name? I was sure I had. Do you know, I can't remember.'

'Just imagine how happy the poet would be to find out that you don't even know who he or she is. What do you think it means?'

'Oh, I don't know. No idea. I just liked the sound of the words,' said Leda.

'Me too.'

'Maybe because it reminds me of me. And of Lucas, of course.'

Zoe rolled her eyes dramatically.

And what about Lucas? He was just the same old Lucas, joking around with everyone, always wanting to have fun.

Is it possible that all boys think about is playing? Zoe found herself thinking. *As soon as the bell rings for break, they dash outside and start kicking balls, throwing balls, catching balls.*

'It's a boy thing,' Leda said to Zoe when she wondered out loud what exactly it was about boys and games.

'Said the wise woman,' Zoe replied. They both laughed and went out to play as well, because it was spring after all, and it was nice to be outside in the sunshine.

During the next lesson, Madame Olenska didn't yell at anyone and she didn't pay anyone any compliments. She just gave looks that were so well aimed you could practically feel them hitting you. Her expression was strangely inscrutable though, so you didn't know whether to be pleased she'd looked at you (*She looked at me, so if she didn't say anything, that must mean I'm doing well. I am doing well, aren't I?*) or worried (*She looked at me, so I must have made a real mess of that, she expects me to do better than that, oh, why isn't she looking at me now that I am doing better?*).

Fortunately, Gimenez was there too. Sometimes the class were on their own with her – if someone came from the secretary's office to fetch Madame Olenska for an emergency, for example. Before Gimenez came along, no one would have dared to interrupt one of Madame's lessons, for fear of being incinerated by her fearful gaze. But now that Gimenez was there, exercises could continue even without Madame and when she left the room, following the agitated secretary, it felt as though the atmosphere relaxed a little, as though everyone gave a tiny, silent sigh of relief. Gimenez was generous with her praise, or rather *geneross*, as she would pronounce it. She was very generous – *geneross* – with the help that she gave the girls too. When they were all holding on to the barre with two hands and lifting themselves up on to the tips of their pointe shoes she went from one girl to the next, turning knees, straightening backs, imperceptibly changing the position of heels with a gentle push of the hand. 'Like thiss. You do it like thiss,' she said. She would stand between two of them, wearing her wonderful red satin shoes, and bend, and straighten, and bend again. When you watched her it felt as though you suddenly understood everything. *A-ha, I see! That's so easy. Wait a moment and I'll do it myself, like this, like this, isn't that right?* And usually it was. Gimenez nodded and smiled her glossy magazine smile, so white and red it almost seemed fake. It was like a flag unfurling as a declaration of victory. 'See, you can do it! You've done it. Hurray!'

In the changing room, Haydée had confessed that she would give anything to have a pair of red shoes like the ones that Gimenez wore. 'With a black tutu like Odile's in *Swan Lake*, and black tights, and a red belt around my waist. What do you think? Wouldn't that look elegant?'

'Too flashy,' Laila said. She was massaging her feet with her special cream. It was so secret that she'd taken the label off the container so that no one else could go out and buy it. It had a menthol smell and reminded Zoe of nasty winter colds. Laila said that the cream toughened her skin and it was true that she was the only one who hadn't suffered any blisters yet. Francine's feet had even bled a bit, but that was only because she'd popped a big blister, so it was nothing too dramatic or scary. No one had lost any toenails or had any wounds that wouldn't heal or that kept on gushing blood or anything gruesome like that. None of the drama they'd anticipated had come to pass, but they were treading very carefully in their new pointe shoes.

When Madame Olenska came back from the secretary's office, she didn't say a word. She just scrutinised them all with her piercing gaze, which wasn't revealing anything at all. Was that possible? That

Madame Olenska of all people had nothing to say? Zoe had the feeling that they were all being examined as much as ever, probably even more, and that Madame Olenska's silence was all about her desire to study exactly how they were developing. Was it a menacing silence, like the deep, almighty silence of lightning flashing across the sky before the thunder came, deafening and violent? No. That wasn't the way Zoe felt. She was calm and serene, not apprehensive like she was when she felt a storm approaching. She knew Madame Olenska was a fair person, someone who did not judge lightly. She also knew it was no longer enough to make an effort, and to work hard. The time was coming when they would have to demonstrate that they had talent, if indeed they actually had any. But talent is something that you can't buy and you can't study. Either you've got it or you haven't.

'Do I have talent?' Zoe asked her reflection in the mirror. She didn't answer, because thoughts were enough when you were talking to yourself. She felt it was strange that there was nothing in the whole world that she was more passionate about than dance. All of the other girls – well, nearly all of them, except for Laila, but she wasn't an example you'd want to imitate – had another interest that they were passionate about. Leda loved clothes, Anna and Paula loved boys and romance. Alissa knew everything there was to know about insects, as Zoe had recently found out when she'd told them loads of details about the life of dragonflies after one had slipped into the classroom through an open window, and the poor thing had caused an unnecessary panic. Sophie was mad about football. She was the only girl who could hold her own with the boys when they had their endless post-match discussions on Monday mornings. *What about me?* thought Zoe. *Aren't I interested in anything? Nothing at all? What if ballet turns out to be a dead end? What am I going to do with my life?* Just the thought of having to start all over again, after having devoted so much time to one single thing paralysed her. She'd had enough of the silence now. The Zoe in the mirror didn't have any answers to her questions. She needed to find someone who did.

Zoe's gran trickled a spoonful of clear honey into her own cup of tea.

'Don't you want some too?' she asked Zoe every time, and every time Zoe replied that she liked tea without sugar or honey, with just a drop of milk, and her gran always said, 'Of course. You're sweet enough already.' She said exactly the same this time too. It was all part of their ritual, Zoe thought with a little smile.

The delicate tinkling of the cup against the saucer (it was part of a beautiful set of Wedgwood porcelain in a soft periwinkle blue, decorated with white figures in

Greek tunics) was the perfect accompaniment for an important, female conversation. Gran understood such things instinctively and she'd laid the table beautifully, with a white lace tablecloth, tiny matching napkins and two silver plates piled high with little golden biscuits that shouted 'Butter! Butter!' at you as soon as you looked at them. Little sugared violets and rose petals poked out here and there among the biscuits, along with candied mint leaves covered with a veil of sugar crystals. There were also silver teaspoons, a silver sugar bowl – which looked like an old-fashioned bathtub with funny little animal feet – and a round blue teapot that was radiating warmth like a fire. It was raining outside and the weather was cooler, so the tea was very welcome.

'Gran, do you think I have any talent as a dancer?' Zoe said straightaway, without wasting any time. While she waited for her gran to answer, she had a sip of her tea and tried to look casual and relaxed. The tea was a little too hot, but bearable, and it was delicious, with a slightly smoky aroma.

'Well, as far as I know, yes you do,' her gran answered without even having to think about it. 'You're passionate. You enjoy it. You're doing well. You know, when you were little, everyone said you looked like a ballerina – and I mean when you were really small, a long time before you went to school to study ballet. I suppose there are certain things that you just have inside you.'

'And do you think I have any talent for anything else? I mean, if everything went wrong at the Academy, what do you think I could do instead?'

This time, her gran thought before answering. 'I'd say that you like looking at what's going on around you. When you were tiny, you always looked down at the ground whenever we went to the park, and you'd come home with your pockets full of little treasures: a shiny stone that had fallen out of a little girl's ring, a plastic doll, a bracelet made of beads. They were things that only you saw. You were good at playing alone. You invented entire worlds with just a twig and a few leaves. Now I don't know exactly what that means, but I don't think you need to worry about the future. Even if you did discover that dance wasn't suitable for you or that you weren't suitable for dance, you still have so much time to decide. At your age most other children still haven't chosen anything at all. The school you go to has forced you to grow up more quickly, in some ways. So if you were to slow down a little, that wouldn't be a bad thing. Are you worried about it?'

'No,' Zoe said, and it was an honest answer. 'It was just something I'd been thinking about a bit. Just a little worry. That's all.'

'Well, don't get yourself all worked up about nothing. Honestly, it's not worth it. Real worries come and find us without us going out looking for them. Sometimes I wish you were a little less serious. A bit more . . . carefree. Like Sara. Or like Maria. Or Leda, although lately she sometimes seems to be a bit care*less*, rather than care*free*. She's away with the fairies, that one.'

Zoe couldn't help but smile. 'Let's just say she's got some worries of her own. Of a different kind.'

'Boys,' her gran said, with a firm nod, and they burst out laughing. The tea had cooled down, so Zoe could drink it without burning her tongue. She drank it slowly, enjoying the flavour. The butter biscuits were calling out to her. She took one, two, three of them. They melted deliciously on her tongue.

'You're going to turn me into a butterball,' Zoe said to her gran.

'You? You're a stick insect,' she replied. 'Do try a mint leaf though. They're delicious.'

Indeed they were. The taste was a little unusual – like a summer garden in the early evening, a shiver on her tongue. Zoe and her gran ate up all of the biscuits and some of the garden too!

After school a few days later, Zoe was walking along the upstairs corridor. There didn't seem to be anyone around, but she'd left her legwarmers in the classroom and thought she'd fetch them before they ended up in the lost-property box. She really liked her legwarmers and they were new, so she'd have been upset to see them crumpled up and lumped together with old shoes, ribbons and belts, and all the other abandoned things.

The door to the classroom where they'd had their lesson was half open. Zoe went in without knocking, because she didn't realise anyone was in the room. Then she saw Mariah Simone! She was dancing, on her own, without music. Zoe flattened herself against the wall. She wished she could just vanish. Mariah Simone was a former student at the Academy and she was now principal dancer at the Academy Theatre. All the girls wanted to be just like her. Who knew, perhaps one day with a bit of luck and lots of talent, they might be.

She was dancing without music, but it was as though she had the music inside her and she was radiating it all around with her perfect movements. She was wearing a very simple, black leotard, the kind with three-quarter-length sleeves, which can look like old sacks on little girls, but look more graceful and elegant depending on how graceful and elegant the wearer is. On Mariah Simone, it was very elegant. Zoe marvelled at the firm softness of her arms, the noble line of her neck, the grace of her perfectly angled head. She was enchanted just by the way she looked, even more so than by the intricate series of rapid steps she tapped out with her shoes. Then she looked down at Mariah's feet, and saw that the rumour was true – her shoes were ancient, grey, worn out and shapeless. But Zoe thought they were beautiful, because they'd clearly done their duty, and that was how they'd ended up in that state; they'd served their owner well, so well that she was reluctant to part with them. After a dizzying sequence of *fouettés*, Mariah Simone made a perfect stop in front of the mirror. She wasn't even breathing heavily, but she should have been. Her control was so good that she didn't show the slightest sign of physical exertion. She had a gentle smile on her face. It was just a mere hint of a smile, nothing like those huge, dazzling smiles that ballerinas usually display at the end of their sequences of pirouettes, as if to say, 'See how good I am?' as thunderous applause drowns out the music.

'Hello,' Mariah Simone said to Zoe, folding her arms. 'What's your name?'

'Zoe,' she answered quietly.

'Hello, Zoe. What are you doing here?'

'I was looking for . . . those,' said Zoe, who had spotted her legwarmers by the wall beside her usual barre position. 'I forgot them. When I was in here earlier.'

'I was just practising without music. Sometimes it helps me to relax. I can feel the music inside. It feels the same as listening to it, but sometimes I like to dance in silence.'

'I can understand that,' was Zoe's only response.

'Well, I'd better get back to it. Would you like to stay for a while?' Mariah Simone asked her.

'I'd love to,' Zoe answered.

'You might as well make yourself comfortable then. Why don't you sit down?' And without another word, she started her silent and solitary dance again, with an audience of one – a young girl who was just as solitary and silent in her own way. Zoe would keep this meeting secret – it was a precious and unique moment just for herself.

When she went back to the changing room to get her things, Zoe took her phone out of her bag and found three messages from Leda. They all said the same thing: *Where r u?* Zoe called her right away and fortunately she didn't need to invent some excuse for her disappearance, because Leda bombarded her with words. After all that silence, it left Zoe feeling rather dazed. She couldn't pay proper attention, and Leda kept saying 'Do you understand?' as though she were talking to someone who spoke a different language. And, in fact, Zoe did feel slightly as though she'd just arrived from another planet, where silence was important. If you really listened, she realised, silence could tell you a lot of things.

CHAPTER SEVEN

A Peculiar
Performance

'What did you say this piece was called?'

'Shh, I'll tell you afterwards.'

Zoe and Roberto were sitting next to each other in the concert hall at Roz's music school and listening to the performance. The hall was packed and the audience was mainly made up of proud and anxious parents. Lots of the dads were armed with video cameras and they'd taken up residence on chairs arranged in a circle around the edge of the hall. They'd carefully covered the seats with newspaper and then climbed up on to them, tall and invisible behind their cameras, ready for their turn to capture the most precious moments of their children's performance. It was a very serious event, Roz had said. The children from the junior years weren't taking part, so that meant you avoided the torture of lots of very short pieces played excruciatingly slowly, or the sudden panic attacks that resulted in instant paralysis of the fingers or floods of tears. Only the older students were in the evening's show and they weren't at all nervous. In fact, they were really keen to show everyone what they could do. Zoe could understand that very well: now that she'd got over the anxiety of her first few years at school, she found the end-of-year recital an absolute pleasure.

After a somewhat peculiar solo on the oboe – what a strange name for an instrument and what a strange sound it made! – and a delicate piano piece for two players, which Zoe recognised as part of Ravel's *Ma mère l'oye*, performed by two fluttery, blonde girls who could have been sisters, it was the turn of Roz and her sax.

It was great watching Roz hugging the sax and rocking it as she played. It actually felt as though she was just letting the instrument sing, as if it was separate from her and had its own will. It was as if the music was already inside the sax, just waiting to be set free by the right movement of fingers, by the right way of closing your eyes and abandoning yourself to the emotion. The music was melancholy and plaintive. Zoe watched Roz for a while, then closed her eyes and just listened. She found it easy to imagine a rainy night, clear and chilly, in some American city or other, with empty sidewalks, alleys full of trashcans and a couple of neon signs flashing in the darkness, on, off, on, off. She felt a sense of solitude, but also a magical sense of possibility. It was a mysterious night when anything might happen.

When the lights came back on for the interval, Zoe was slightly disappointed to discover that it wasn't a mysterious night at all. In fact, it was just a calm and pleasant evening. She and Roberto stood up and went to stretch their legs in the music school's large and elegant foyer. It had wood panelling and tall mirrors that reflected each other, multiplying the view and the people who were chatting and looking around, smiling and nodding. The dads with video cameras eagerly checked to make sure their recordings were perfect and the mums formed little groups and chatted away.

'It's called *Almost Blue*,' Zoe said to Roberto, glancing through the programme.

'I think I've heard it before. Don't you think it would be great to choreograph a ballet for that music?'

'A *pas de deux*,' Zoe said.

'Yes, but the two dancers are separate, they just brush

against each other without ever really touching and dance the same steps without dancing them together – as if they're searching for one another, but don't know how to find each other.'

'And they'd be dressed in blue. Well, in almost blue. You know, in those one-piece suits with long sleeves.'

'Ooh, listen to the costume designer at work,' Roberto joked.

'Says the choreographer!' Zoe shot straight back at him, smiling.

The second half was far more wild and exciting than the first. It was as though whoever had designed the programme had decided, *Okay, that's enough of that, we've been serious so far, now we're really going to let our hair down.* It started with a drum solo to make you tap your feet, then a piano joined in, then it was the turn of the bass, and then came the sax. The music was pulsating, lively, and unpredictable. 'They're improvising,' Roberto whispered in Zoe's ear. Roz threw her head back and lifted up the sax. It was a blaze of light in the darkness of the hall. *She's really enjoying herself,* thought Zoe, with a smile.

When they'd finished, it seemed as though the applause would never stop. Looking around, Zoe had the feeling that people weren't just clapping to be polite, but that the audience had really enjoyed the show, even the grannies with their salt-and-pepper hair, and even the mums who looked so calm and collected on the outside. The audience wasn't just clapping because of their affection for the performers. Zoe had enjoyed herself too; she was glad that she'd come. It seemed to confirm one of the things she'd been thinking about recently: that real friends don't need to see each other every day, or to talk twice a week. They're always there and you know where to find them when you need them, and vice versa, of course. That was true of Alice and of Roz.

When Roz came out to meet them, she was boiling hot, but glowing with happiness. Her very blond hair was in a bit of a mess, her cheeks were bright pink in contrast with the rest of her skin and her eyes were shining even more than usual.

'Did you like it?' she asked them. They both nodded and smiled.

'You were great,' Roberto said. 'I'd really like you to accompany me when I dance one day.' Zoe looked at him in surprise. It was a really good idea. It must just have come to him, because he hadn't said anything to her about it.

Roz nodded enthusiastically. 'Yeah, wonderful. I'd love to. Really.'

The pianist from the second half of the show came over to join them. He was older than them and very skinny, with long black hair hanging down around his thin face. 'Do you want to come for a drink? We're going to the music hall bar to have a drink to celebrate.'

Zoe and Roberto looked at each other.

Roz answered for all of them. 'I'll go and ask my mum and dad if it's okay. We came with them.'

'Okay,' the skinny boy said and then he introduced himself to Zoe and Roberto. 'Hi, I'm Paul.'

After they'd all said their hellos, Roz came back with a yes from her parents. 'Mum and Dad have said they'll go for a bit of a walk. They'll come back and pick us up in forty-five minutes.'

Paul pulled a face. 'That's not very long. But I suppose you're only little, aren't you? Come on, let's hurry up, so you can make the most of your brief taste of freedom. The others have gone already.'

A few minutes later, they were making their way into the music hall's atmospherically lit bar. As they passed the man behind the counter, Paul said hi to him. He nodded back. 'Hi, Paul. I see you've brought a few little chums with you.' The way he said it was friendly, not mean, but Zoe still felt vaguely uncomfortable.

Paul and Roz's friends, the older musicians, were sitting on low padded seats around a huge square table. They'd already ordered drinks and Paul introduced the new arrivals to the group. Zoe said hi and heard six names in rapid succession, then found she couldn't remember even one of them a moment later. The others squeezed up so that they could sit down. Zoe got the seat right on the end. It was really just a corner of the bench with a cushion that kept slipping on to the floor, so she had to hold on tight.

'What are you having?' Paul asked. 'My treat. And you can have whatever you like. The barman's my brother's mate.'

'Erm . . . just a tonic water,' Zoe said, slightly intimidated.

'Oh, come on. That's for little kids,' Paul said. 'I'll get you something nice.' He went off to place an order at the bar. When he came back, he nodded to Zoe to move up a bit to make room for him, then sat too close to her on the increasingly precarious cushion. He smelled strange, like unwashed hair. She looked at Roberto for help, but there were three people between them and he was squashed in between Roz and one of the blond pianists, so he couldn't do anything. Paul leaned towards her and asked, 'Do you play an instrument?'

'No,' Zoe said, 'I'm studying classical dance.' But her answer was lost because Paul was handing out the drinks. He passed Zoe a tall, cylindrical glass, full of something orange, with a straw poking out of the top and a mint leaf floating on the surface. Paul nodded at her to try it and she did as she was told. It was good. It looked like orange juice, but there was something else in there that she didn't recognise. It was a little strong on her tongue, but it wasn't unpleasant.

'What were you saying?' Paul said, making another attempt at communication. He'd ordered the same drink and had already downed half of it in two gulps.

'I'm studying classical . . .' Zoe repeated, but this time it was Roz who interrupted her, by coming over and whispering in her ear, 'I'm going to the loo. Will you come with me?' She pulled Zoe by the hand, forcing her to stand up.

The loo was tiny and decorated entirely in blue. Roz looked at herself in the mirror, turned on the tap and put her wrists under the jet of cold water.

'The heat in there's going to make me explode,' she said. And then, still looking herself in the eyes, she added, 'Don't trust Paul. And don't drink that stuff he got you. There's alcohol in it. It's not good for you.'

So that explained the mystery of the strong taste.

'But it didn't taste like it,' Zoe said, feeling as though she had to defend herself.

'You're right. It doesn't,' Roz said. 'But the alcohol goes straight to your head and makes you feel really weird.'

'Sounds as though you're speaking from experience,' Zoe said, trying to catch her friend's eye in the mirror.

'I am,' Roz said. 'Paul's a genius on the piano, but

you really have to keep your eye on him.'

'So why did we have to go for a drink with him? We could have just gone straight home, couldn't we? Or come to the bar by ourselves, with your mum and dad.'

'There's a problem,' Roz said, biting her bottom lip. She wasn't all pink and white like a fairytale princess now; her face was pale. 'The problem is that I'm in love with him. So I always do whatever he says. I know I shouldn't. I know it's wrong and that I'm messing up, but I can't help it. It's stronger than I am.'

'Oh,' was all that came to Zoe's lips.

'Come on. Let's go back to the others. We don't have much time before they come and pick us up, because we have to go to beddy-byes like good little children. I bet Paul will stay out for another few hours though. He says he's meeting some friends at a club in town.'

'How old is he?' Zoe asked her. She couldn't believe anyone of their age had that much freedom.

'Sixteen. Ancient, eh?' Roz gave a bitter laugh and tidied the curls around her face.

'Well, yes, a bit,' Zoe admitted. 'Erm . . . he's a bit old for you. I mean, you're only thirteen.'

'Roberto's quite young, isn't he?'

'He's twelve, same as me.'

'Exactly. The two of you are practically babies. I don't even know why I'm talking to you about this stuff. I don't think you could possibly understand.'

'No,' Zoe said, very quietly, so quietly that Roz didn't even hear her. She dried her hands, opened the door and left. Zoe followed her, because she didn't have any other option.

Fortunately, Roz's parents were already waiting for them, discreetly perched on two high stools at the bar.

'Let's go,' Zoe said to Roberto, without even sitting down. Roz had moved to what had been Zoe's place before, close to Paul. He hadn't even turned to look at her. He was chatting with one of the two blondes. It was difficult to tell which one it was – they looked almost exactly the same. He'd already emptied his glass.

'We're going,' Roberto announced, having made his way over to Zoe by climbing over quite a few pairs of outstretched legs.

Paul looked up at them, a little annoyed at having been interrupted. Then he noticed that Zoe's glass was still almost full, and said, 'Do you mind if I finish this? It's a shame to let good things go to waste.'

'Go ahead,' Zoe said. She took Roberto's arm and they went over to where Roz's parents were sitting. Roz sighed, then stood up and joined them.

There was a strange, awkward silence in the car on the way home. Roberto was the first stop, followed by Zoe. She tapped Roz on the elbow to say goodbye. Roz just gave her a tight smile, then turned to look out of the window.

'Night. Thanks for the lift,' Zoe said to Roz's parents, as she slid out of the car, with a sense of relief.

Later, when she was in bed, she texted Roberto. *Did you drink it?*

No. Smelled gin. Bleurgh! :p

Prefer whisky? Zoe texted back, feeling a little happier.

Ha ha. Night, Z.

She thought back over the evening and the mixture of contrasting emotions she'd felt: first the pure joy of listening to good music, then the sense of excitement at doing something new and different – going for a drink in the evening, with friends, which was the kind of thing that grown-ups did – then the weird atmosphere and her worries about Roz, who seemed really confused and not at all happy. It had been a strange, different kind of evening and a bit scary too. Zoe wondered what would have happened if she'd drunk all of that big orange drink. Probably nothing, but she might have been ill, or maybe she'd have started giggling like an idiot – alcohol seemed to have that effect on people. Before it made you ill, of course.

What about Roz? She'd phone her tomorrow. She'd try to understand. No, not tomorrow. Maybe the day after. First she needed to think about it for a while.

Otherwise she wouldn't know what to say to her. Should she tell her to forget about Paul? That was obviously the last thing Roz wanted to hear, and the last thing she wanted to do. So what could Zoe do to help her? Maybe all she could do was listen. Yes, that was exactly what she'd do.

CHAPTER EIGHT

A Few Sweets Can Work Wonders

'And three, and four. *Battement tendu*, come along. Maestro Fantin, would you like to try that Bartók we chose? Thank you . . .'

The lesson today felt unusual. It was strange how all it took was a change of music to make every movement, even the ones you were really used to, feel completely different. Maestro Fantin definitely seemed to be inspired by the music. You could tell by the way his locks of white hair bounced around as he hit the keys. So much energy! There was a lot of power surging through the music, which seemed to be some sort of country dance. Zoe really liked it. She found it easy to get involved in the exercises. It was much easier than lessons had been recently.

Madame Olenska had of course noticed that everyone was feeling restless. It was something to do with the atmosphere and the time of year. It was getting into their heads and all the way into their muscles, making them feel unfocused, fidgety and disobedient. She'd spoken to them about it a couple of days before. 'I understand if you're feeling tired. The end of the school year is approaching and you've had a lot of things to cope with. There was my absence, and then boys and girls had to split up and the girls started dancing *en pointe*. I have to say that you've dealt very well with all of these changes, but we certainly can't afford to let things slide now. Not with the end-of-year recital and the exams coming up. Try to eat plenty of fresh fruit and vegetables – you need lots of real vitamins. No supplements or pills, please. Try to lead a healthy life both inside and outside of school, and concentrate on your work. I'll do everything I can to help you.'

Zoe could feel Madame Olenska's help and support in the music she and Maestro Fantin had chosen for the class too. It was strange, but somehow the music made her feel so much better and more focused. Zoe had often thought that Madame Olenska had a talent for magic. Perhaps she'd cast a spell that only worked in her classroom. As soon as she got back to the changing room after class, Zoe felt listless and a bit tired again.

To cheer herself up, she decided to make a detour instead of going straight home. Her detour took her to the costume-making department and to Demetra's workroom. Zoe knocked on the door, waited for Demetra to call 'Come in!', then pushed open the door. She said hello to her friend and collapsed on an empty armchair. A split second later, she leaped to her feet, rubbing her leg.

'Found a pin?' Demetra said with a smile. 'Give it here. We don't want to injure any star ballerinas who happen to pass through, do we?'

Cautiously, Zoe felt around for the culprit and managed to locate it without stabbing herself again. She stuck it into one of the pincushions lined up on Demetra's worktable. Then she dropped back down on to the safe armchair and rested her cheek on her hand, thoughtful and exhausted.

'Tired, eh? Why don't you have one of these? That'll make you feel better,' Demetra said, holding out her famous tin of sweets, which was always full to the brim with all kinds of unusual goodies, which Demetra discovered in some obscure sweetshop, and only handed out to people she really, really liked. Zoe was amazed that the level of sweets in the tin never seemed to go down. Demetra probably topped them up every day, aware that an overflowing tin of sweets made a very different impression than a half-empty one. Zoe chose an old-fashioned sort of sweet, or at least the wrapper looked old-fashioned. It was white, with swirling words written on it in gold writing and the colour of the flavour filling in the loops of the words. *The colour of the flavour* – what a nice thought. Of course, it was true that every flavour had its own colour. Zoe had chosen a ratafia-flavoured sweet, whatever ratafia was. According to the wrapper, it was a pretty shade of ruby red. 'A good choice. They're my favourites,' nodded Demetra. Then, anticipating Zoe's question, she said, 'Ratafia was a drink that ladies used to sip in the old days. Would you like a few more, to take with you for later?'

'Ooh, yes please,' Zoe said.

'But don't eat them all at once, eh? Make them last.'

Zoe tucked her supply of sweets into her pocket and unwrapped the first one and popped it into her mouth. Her tongue agreed with the wrapper: it was a red flavour. Quite a dark red. There was silence while Zoe sucked her sweet, and Demetra sat at her worktable, sewing a string of green sequins around the neckline of a bodice with a short, stiff tutu attached. Finally, Zoe regained the power of speech.

'A friend of mine really likes this boy who's no good for her,' she said. She quickly explained the situation to Demetra, who listened without taking her eyes off her work, only interrupting Zoe with a few words such as 'oh' and 'ah' and 'I see'. Then there was a long pause. Zoe's sweet, which had been quite sizeable to start with, had by now been transformed into a thin sheet of sugar. Zoe couldn't resist biting it. As it gave a satisfying crack, Demetra finally said, 'I don't think there's much you can do about it. If she doesn't understand that he's no good for her . . . Actually, I think she probably already knows, but she needs to find the strength to forget about him and move on, and that's something only she can do. It's not something you can help her with.'

Zoe nodded, feeling vaguely relieved. She'd already suspected that there wasn't much she could do to help Roz – nothing really practical anyway. Hearing Demetra say the same thing made her feel calmer and less responsible. So she was right to think that all she could offer Roz was her friendship and a listening ear. That was okay. Thank goodness.

'And how are things going with the new shoes?' Demetra asked her.

'Oh, pretty well. At least they're not hurting. Madame Olenska and Gimenez are taking things slowly.'

'I know. It's not as if there's any hurry, anyway. You're already ahead of schedule. How are the others coping?'

'Some better than others,' Zoe answered. She told her about Leda, who seemed even taller when she danced *en pointe*, and about Francine, who had heard that rubbing alcohol hardens the skin, so she'd started carrying a little pink plastic bottle of it everywhere she went, the way the others carried bottles of water. She kept dabbing the alcohol on her feet with cotton wool, so the changing room smelled like a hospital. She told her about Sophie who kept bursting into tears, but always out of sight of Madame Olenska, because she couldn't bear people making a fuss. Sophie said it was all too difficult and her shoes wouldn't bend properly and she was sure they were never going to. She told her about Laila, who kept trying to break in her shoes by hitting them and bending them against hard surfaces. And she told her about the boys, who sometimes, when they'd finished their character dance lessons, tiptoed in to watch the girls, as though they were an alien species. It probably felt a bit strange for them, because until a few weeks ago they'd all done the same things together. The boys and the girls were starting to be very different and it was a bit unsettling for everyone.

Demetra just sewed and nodded and said 'hmmm' every now and then.

'I wonder how many times you've heard all these stories before,' Zoe said. 'I bet everyone has the same problems year after year. It must be so boring for you. Do tell me if I'm being boring. I don't like to think that I might be boring.' Then, to stop herself from talking, she unwrapped another sweet and started sucking it.

'Sweetheart, you're not boring,' Demetra said after a while, when she'd finished sewing on the sequins. She tied the thread, snipped it off, stuck the needle into one of her pincushions and held up the tutu to consider the final result.

'What a dreadful colour,' she muttered, almost to herself. 'It doesn't look good on anyone. Still, it's for Julia Monda. She'll look like a zombie.' Zoe knew that Demetra thought that Julia Monda, one of Mariah Simone's fellow dancers, was a nasty piece of work.

Demetra couldn't stand her, even though she was a good dancer. But she'd do anything, including making a tutu from scratch in just two hours, for Mariah Simone.

'No, you're not boring,' Demetra repeated, going back to the previous conversation as though nothing had happened. 'It's different for everyone. And it's new for all of you. So the stories may be a little similar, but they're not exactly the same as anything that's happened before. Did you know that when Monda and Simone were little, Monda was the better dancer of the two? Simone was so fragile and she was often ill. The poor thing was as thin as a rake. When she put on her pointe shoes, her feet looked huge and completely out of proportion. She used to cry sometimes too, but she did it in secret, because she was so proud. No one would ever have bet a penny on her doing so brilliantly. That other one used to go around with her nose in the air like a princess, as though she were the only one capable of dancing on the tips of her toes, but then, of course, the tables turned. Of course, Monda's still good, but Simone? Now, she's got that sacred flame. Inside her, I mean.'

A sacred flame . . . Zoe tried to imagine what that might look like. Inside her heart, or somewhere near. She pictured one of those bronze lamps that they used in ancient Greece or Rome, the kind you see in films, which lit up as if by magic. She wondered if it was possible to have just a lamp inside, without any flames. *Do I have a lamp inside me?* Zoe wondered. *Is it lit? How do you find out?*

She decided to have a third sweet, another ratafia. It felt dark red on her tongue and inside her cheeks. While she ate it in silence, she let her thoughts wander, until, finally, her head felt empty and light. She turned to look at the costumes that were hanging around the walls. Then she started thinking about colours and the sparkle and the frothy glamour of the tutus and the empty, light feeling disappeared.

'Say hello to your friend Alissa from me,' Demetra said unexpectedly. She was leaning over the table now, cutting out a coral-coloured bodice with extreme precision.

'Alissa? I didn't know . . .' Zoe said, feeling slightly jealous.

'No, don't worry. I'm not that close to her, not like I am with you.' Demetra could read Zoe like a book. 'But I do think she's a nice girl. She's been very brave. Now that she's stopped wearing those garish colours, she looks a lot nicer too.'

'You're right,' Zoe said. 'She's nice inside as well.'

'That's a kind thing to say, sweetheart,' Demetra said. 'Now, you should scoot off home, before they lock you in.'

Zoe ate the last sweet when she was on the bus. It lasted exactly the length of the journey. Zoe felt much, much better now. Was it Demetra? Or was it the magical powers of the sweets? Ultimately, they were both the same thing.

That night, she wrote in her notebook again.

A real ballerina must have that inner flame. How do you ignite it? Can someone else light it for you? Are you born with a spark already inside you? Or does someone give you that spark? It's a mystery.

CHAPTER NINE

Names are Funny Things

Zoe was walking down the corridor, going from one lesson to the next. She was on her own and she was just thinking how nice it was to spend time alone sometimes. You could relax, think about things and then afterwards you were all the happier to see other people again. Then she heard someone coming up behind her. They gave her a gentle tap on the shoulder and then walked beside her. So, she wasn't on her own anymore.

It was Alex, a boy in the top year at school, who was a very good dancer and very nice too. He worked as an usher in the Academy Theatre to earn a little money.

Quite a few of the older students had jobs at the theatre. Most of them worked as ushers, but others worked in the café or in the shop that sold books, programmes, CDs, postcards and other souvenirs from one of the most famous theatres in the world.

'How are you doing?' he asked Zoe, looking down at her. He was very tall. He had black hair and brown eyes, and pale skin with freckles on his cheeks and nose. *A bit like me,* Zoe thought.

'Fine, thanks.' She was already worring about what to say next. She didn't know Alex very well – in fact, it was the first time she'd ever spoken to him – so what could she really ask him?

It wasn't a problem. 'So, how are you getting on with dancing *en pointe*?' asked Alex, straightaway.

Zoe smiled, but it felt more like a grimace. 'Oh, you know,' she said. 'It's still early days and I haven't got used to it yet. I suppose it's going quite well. I mean, we're not doing anything really difficult yet, but I'm a bit nervous about the thought that it's only going to get harder.'

'I know. Then again, it's always worse waiting for new things to start than it is when you're actually doing them. Once you get down to it, you usually find that everything's possible with a bit of effort, but all the waiting can really be a strain.'

Zoe thought he might be referring to himself: he had his diploma exam coming up soon. Alex was bound to pass with top marks, but what would he do then? Would he join the Academy's own dance company or would he do other auditions, perhaps for one of the major companies abroad? She felt a little nervous, but overcame her doubts and decided to ask him. 'So, do you know what you're going to do when you leave school?'

'Ha! That's exactly what I was just thinking about. I've no idea. I'd like a change of scene, maybe try my luck and see if I enjoy living on my own in a different city, preferably somewhere abroad. You know, I want to stretch myself, and not just in dancing.' He looked into her eyes, slowing his pace, and Zoe slowed down too. 'Maybe it all seems too far off for you, but you understand, don't you?'

'Yes,' Zoe answered, and it was an honest response, even though she'd never really thought about leaving home before. She was fairly certain that it would happen one day, because everyone leaves home, sooner or later, and everyone wants to discover what life elsewhere has to offer.

At that point they went their separate ways. 'I'm going upstairs,' Alex said, nodding in the direction of the stairs to the rehearsal rooms.

'And I'm going downstairs,' Zoe said. The language labs were down in the basement.

'Okay. See you later. It's been nice chatting,' he said, giving her that tap on the shoulder again. Zoe wasn't quite sure she liked it: it made her feel a bit like a pet dog.

Whether it was meant as the kind of pat you'd give a dog or as something else, Leda didn't miss it. She ran halfway up the stairs to meet Zoe and said, 'Well, well, well, Zoe, aren't you a dark horse? I didn't know you went for older men. I mean, of course, Alex is cute . . .'

'Don't be such an idiot, Leda,' Zoe replied, with a smile in her voice, because she was secretly flattered that Leda might think such a silly thing, even though it wasn't the slightest bit true.

'Idiot? You call me an idiot just because I caught you with your new boyfriend?' Leda teased. 'I can't imagine why you haven't told me all about him . . .'

'Because there's nothing to say.'

'So, have the two of you been seeing each other for long? The way he was talking to you, it all looked very cosy . . .'

That was the point when Zoe could have said, when Zoe *should* have said, that it really was the first time Alex had ever spoken a word to her, except for the occasional hello. But she didn't.

Later, in the language lab, she noticed that Leda kept looking at her with a mixture of curiosity and suspicion. When the lesson was over and they were heading back to their classroom, Leda started talking about Alex again. 'I mean, yes, he's cute. Don't like the name much though. Alex, Alex. No, not very romantic. And you can't tell whether it's a boy or a girl.' Then she giggled and went over to whisper something in Sophie's ear.

Later, at home, in the hour between homework and dinner, which was Zoe's favourite time of the day, because her time was her own then, she found herself thinking about names. She quite liked the name Alex. Alexander. She was fairly sure it was Greek. Zoe was a Greek name too. It meant 'life' and it was quite an unusual name. She was the only Zoe she knew. Leda was another name from faraway, from Greek mythology. Some of the other girls in the class had pretty, musical names: Francine, Alissa, Estelle. Only Paula, Sophie and Stephanie had names she didn't really like. Zoe had always been very happy with her own name, because it was short and had an unusual sound. Not many names began with a Z, like hers. Or ended with an X, like Alex's. If she had a little boy one day, she thought she might call him Zac, but if she had a girl she liked the idea of a pretty name, a sparkly name, something like Stella perhaps. Roberto had a nice ring to it, but most importantly it suited its owner. It was always so strange if someone looked like a Mark, for example, but turned out to be called Guy. Then there were all those dull, neutral names that were more or less interchangeable, like Anne and John. Zoe was glad she didn't have a neutral name. She was sure Alex liked his name too. It was the kind of name you remembered and that was important for a performer. Have you ever heard of a great dancer called John Smith or Anne Jones? Surnames were a different matter, but you had even less choice about your surname than your first name. If you really didn't like your first name, you could at least persuade your friends to call you something else. Your real name could remain a secret between you and your passport. There wasn't much you could do about your surname if it was boring though. And even if it was exotic and glamorous, everyone would get it wrong and you'd have to spell it out all the time.

Then Zoe realised that all that thinking about names was just a way of avoiding thinking about something else – about how bothered she'd been by Leda and her teasing about Alex. Of course, she was pleased that he'd spoken to her and that they'd talked about so many important things in such a short time. It was nice of someone his age to stop and talk to her, especially about such serious matters. It hadn't occurred to her to attach any more importance to their conversation though. There was no way someone his age would like a girl of her age, was there?

During dinner, Zoe's mum immediately noticed something was wrong, but as she was good at being a mum, she didn't say anything. Zoe could just feel the concern in her watchful gaze. Sara was staying over at a friend's, and the house was strangely quiet without all the usual squabbling between Sara and Maria. Her mum said, 'Dad and Maria can clear the table this evening. Zoe, will you come with me to my bedroom? There's something I'd like to show you.'

She really did have something lovely to show to Zoe. She picked up a little pouch made of green gauze and tied with a blue ribbon and took out a beautiful, delicate bracelet with all sorts of little charms attached. They were all connected with spring and summer: two little butterflies made of enamel and jewels, tiny glass cherries with shiny green leaves, a sparkly dragonfly, two minuscule ladybirds, and lots of pretty flowers of all different kinds.

'It's beautiful,' Zoe said, running it through her fingers so she could take a proper look at the individual charms. 'Where did you get it?'

'It was a present. Alexa bought it for me in Paris.'

Alexa was one of her mum's friends. She worked for a fashion magazine and did a lot of travelling. She dressed in the most peculiar clothes, the kind of thing no one else would ever have dared to wear, but they looked good on her.

'But it's not your birthday,' Zoe pointed out.

'That's just the way Alexa is. When she likes something, she buys it for you. She thinks that it's most important for the person who buys the present to like it. I suppose she's right in a way. I'm just worried that the bracelet's a bit fragile and that it'll get caught up in something or that one of the charms will come off. I'll have to be so careful when I'm wearing it. Why don't you try it on?'

Studying a small purple flower with a violet centre and fan-shaped leaves, Zoe said, 'Is Alexa a good friend?'

'Hmmm, a good friend?' her mum said thoughtfully. 'Well, she likes to think about the people she's fond of, so she often buys them presents. She's certainly generous. But being generous isn't just about presents. It's about giving other kinds of things as well, the sort of thing you can't buy. Your time, for example, or your attention.'

'So you're generous then. You give us a lot of your time instead of reading all day, which I'm sure you'd rather do.'

'Or going to the cinema,' her mum added with a smile. Then she said, in a serious voice, 'You know, I don't think I'm really generous as such. I'm a mum. There are some things that just come naturally to you. I'm sure there's more than one way of being a good mum. Everyone has to find their own way.'

'I like your way. I know you noticed I was a bit preoccupied this evening and that's why you called me in here to talk.'

'That's true,' her mum said. 'So, what were you worrying about?'

'Oh, nothing bad. It's just that Leda's been saying I

like one of the older boys at school, someone in the top year. Or maybe she's been saying that he likes me. I'm not quite sure anymore. She's got me all confused.'

'And is it true?' her mum asked.

'No. Well, I haven't ever thought about it really. Until today I only knew his name. He'd never really spoken to me before. And of course he's far too old for me. It's just Leda being silly.'

'So what exactly are you worried about?'

'Actually, I don't really know,' Zoe admitted.

'Well, that's because I don't think you have anything to worry about, so that's why you're all confused. Or maybe you're just annoyed with Leda for sticking her nose into your business.'

'That's what friends usually do, isn't it? Stick their noses in?'

'Only if you let them. You don't have to tell each other everything, just because you're friends. You should be honest, that's true, but you don't have to say everything. It isn't obligatory. You might have one friend you tell everything to and other friends you only tell certain things. There aren't any rules.'

'The problem is that I haven't said anything at all to her about it. I didn't get a chance. Anyway, it's not as if there was anything to say.'

'You feel as though she's invading your privacy, don't you?' Zoe's mum said.

'Yes, that's it. Exactly. She's invading my privacy.'

'You shouldn't feel obliged to tell her all about yourself and what you're thinking. Real friendships give you some freedom, some space to breathe. Growing up is all about finding out who you really are and who your friends are.'

'Otherwise you end up like those girls who dress just the same. They wear the same T-shirts, same jeans, same shoes, even the same belt and make-up.' Zoe nodded to herself. 'There are two girls at school who are like that. They're really scary, just like clones.'

'My point exactly,' agreed her mum. 'I'd steer clear of that kind of thing. It might start off as a bit of fun, but it can become dangerous. You end up without any tastes or interests of your own. You're just the same as someone else.'

'Just the same. Dull, bland, boring. Tell you what though, this bracelet certainly isn't boring,' Zoe said, holding out her wrist so that her mum could undo the bracelet and carefully slip it back into its gauze bag.

'Neither is my friendship with Alexa. I'm so pleased she gave me this present.'

'I understand,' Zoe said. 'Leda would never spend all of that money on a present for me. She might buy it for herself though.'

'Now you mention it, Alexa does have an identical one . . .'

Zoe and her mum laughed and gave each other a hug and a goodnight kiss. Zoe went to the kitchen, where she found her dad and Maria, who had tidied up beautifully, and were now demolishing what was left of the chocolate cake. They were sitting in comfortable silence at the table, with two pretty plates and silver forks. 'Caught you!' she said.

'It's all gone,' Maria replied, talking with a full mouth that had icing and sprinkles all around it.

'Never mind,' Zoe said, leaning down to kiss her dad. She didn't feel at all left out. She'd had her special moment with Mum and now Maria was enjoying her time with Dad. If Sara had been there, it would all have been a little more complicated, but loving each other shouldn't be a competition.

In bed later, Zoe thought about her mum's beautiful bracelet and about the meaning of friendship. Just before she closed her eyes, she realised that she hadn't spent a single moment thinking about Alex – but of course she hadn't, because she realised Alex wasn't the real problem.

CHAPTER TEN

What a Mess

No, Alex wasn't the real problem, but he was certainly about to cause some problems, through no fault of his own. The next morning before class started, Roberto walked over to Zoe's desk, where she was revising for a French grammar test. There was one rule that she just couldn't get into her head. Roberto interrupted her revision and said, 'You and I need to talk.'

'What's up?' Zoe closed her book, saying farewell to the grammar rule, which flew away, happily forgotten, instead of sticking in her memory as it was supposed to.

'No, I mean we really need to talk. Properly. Seriously.'

'What about?' Zoe asked innocently.

'About us.'

Zoe felt a mixture of curiosity and fear at the way Roberto said 'us'. It seemed so ominous, so over the top. But she didn't have a chance to say so, because the bell went for the start of the lesson and their teacher rushed into the classroom and started handing out test sheets.

At breaktime, after the test, which naturally contained a question all about Zoe's least favourite grammar rule, Zoe went out and sat in the playground. Roberto swept down on her like a bird of prey and she suddenly felt like a defenceless mouse with nowhere to hide. Then she breathed deeply and thought to herself, *Have I done anything wrong? Why should I feel guilty?* Her sudden, crystal-clear certainty that she was completely innocent made it easier to face Roberto's searching gaze. He came straight out with it this time. 'Leda says you like someone else.'

Zoe breathed a sigh of relief. She felt like laughing – she should have known it was about Alex. There was no way Leda could resist the temptation of spreading the news and making it a little more interesting, by embroidering it with her own details and turning it into a different story altogether. Yet again, more complications, more arabesques. Unfortunately, Roberto didn't seem to think it was very funny. Zoe could tell that his sense of humour was at an all-time low.

'Yes, well, Leda says a lot of things without thinking first,' Zoe said. 'She saw me talking to Alex in the corridor yesterday and put two and two together, but somehow she managed to turn it into eight.'

'So, if it added up to four, what would that mean?' asked Roberto. 'Why exactly were you talking to Alex?'

'It would mean that it added up to four and no more. I've already told you – I was talking to him and that's all.'

'So, are the two of you getting together? Does he want to go out with you? Has he been sending you love letters?'

Love letters?! Once again, Zoe just felt like laughing. She also felt like thumping Roberto and saying, 'Listen to yourself! Have you gone mad?' At the same time, she was also annoyed. What right did he have to ask her all those questions? More than that, what right did he have to doubt her?

'Listen,' she said to him, and suddenly she felt very serious, more serious than she had ever felt before when she was talking to Roberto. 'Either you believe me or you don't. And if you don't believe me, then I have nothing else to say to you.'

'But we're going out with each other, you and me . . .' he protested. Zoe's confident attitude had obviously made him feel a little insecure.

'What does that mean? That I'm not allowed to talk to any other boys?'

'But . . . But I thought . . .' Roberto was running out of steam. His face was bright red and he looked really upset and Zoe actually felt a little sorry for him.

'What did you think?' she asked him. Her voice sounded more gentle than she'd intended.

'I thought that because your friend Roz has got a thing about that older guy, you might have thought it was a good idea too.'

Zoe threw her head back and snorted with laughter. 'Just because Roz is being stupid, why do you think I have to be stupid too?' She looked away, slightly offended. What on earth was he thinking?

'I . . . I'm sorry,' he stammered. 'It's just that I'm . . . jealous.'

Zoe wanted to laugh again. Jealous? What a big word. What an ugly word. It sounded so grown-up. It sounded like something off a soap opera. As far as Zoe was concerned, it was a stupid emotion. She never felt jealous if Roberto chatted with the other girls. So why should he be jealous of her? She answered the question herself. It's because he's not like me. We're different. We're all different. Sometimes that's nice, but sometimes it causes problems.

'You've absolutely no need to be jealous,' she said to him after a while, looking into his eyes. 'And I don't want you to feel jealous either. We're not in some tragedy by Shakespeare. I want us both to enjoy ourselves and have fun together. Forget all the anxiety. Just trust me. And relax.'

Then the bell went and everyone hurried back to lessons. Zoe took out her book and tried to read it, but nothing would go in. She just kept reading the same sentence over and over and the words didn't seem to make any sense at all. Then again, what Roberto had said didn't make much sense either. She was feeling pretty angry with him. No, not exactly angry, more annoyed, really. She wasn't his property. She was a person. As Zoe saw it, jealousy had more to do with property, with owning things – it's mine, all mine.

She was angry with Leda too. No, not angry exactly. Irritated. With her incredible, innocent thoughtlessness, she must have said just the wrong thing in just the wrong tone of voice. She probably thought it was funny to make Roberto believe something that wasn't true.

That's exactly what Zoe said to Leda when the lesson was over. She managed to keep out of Roberto's way, but took Leda by the arm and steered her to the safety of the girls' toilets. 'So, do you want to tell me why you open your mouth without thinking first? Roberto just caused a real scene. For some reason, he thinks that I'm going out with Alex.'

'And he caused a scene? How romantic,' Leda said, lacing her fingers together and raising her hands to her chest like an old-fashioned actress. 'I told you he really loves you.'

'So, are you going to tell me exactly what you said to him?'

'Me? Nothing. Just that I saw you with Alex, and the two of you seemed really . . .'

'Really what?'

'Really . . . friendly. That's all.'

'You're such an idiot,' Zoe said with a sigh.

'I know,' Leda said happily. 'But at least you know now that he really loves you.'

'Do me a favour, Leda. Stop using such silly words. Love!'

'Why? Don't you think it's real love?'

'No, actually, I don't think it is.'

'So why are the two of you always together?'

'We're not together all the time. I have other things in my life. Other people.'

'Such as . . . Alex?' Leda teased, fluttering her eyelashes.

'Such as you, you idiot.'

'So I'm more important than your boyfriend, am I?'

'That's another word I'd like you to stop using. Please, please, please. Can't you be more like a normal girl? Can't you just act your age?'

'Ha! All of the normal girls our age behave in exactly the same way as I do. You're the odd one out, Zoe. You're not totally weird though, because you do have a boyfriend at least. Then again, you pretend that he's not your boyfriend . . . And you've got loads of boys after you, but you pretend that they're not . . . If you ask me, it's just an act. In actual fact, you're just like me and all of the other girls. You just try to pretend that you're better than everyone else.'

'You know you are seriously, seriously stupid sometimes?' Zoe said to Leda, shaking her head.

'Of course I am,' Leda answered. 'But that's the way it works with friends. There's always an intelligent one and a stupid one. You're the intelligent one, so I have to be the stupid one. There are other variations too – the pretty friend and the plain friend, for example. But that doesn't apply to us, of course, because we're both total babes, but in different ways, so we're not in competition with each other. Imagine if we both had long blond hair and blue eyes. It'd be all-out war. We probably wouldn't even be friends with each other. As it is, though, everything's fine. You want to be careful though. Boys prefer stupid girls. They don't scare them as much. So maybe you should stop being so intellectual or you'll end up on your own and I'll have to throw you a few of my rejects. I don't know why you can't just be honest about it. You and Roberto are going out with each other. You're a couple, and that's that. If he's jealous, that's his problem. Either he's right to be jealous or he's just insecure.'

'Or he's as stupid as you are,' Zoe said, grinning. It could be hard to resist Leda sometimes. She was so silly that you couldn't help but like her.

'Oh, of course, now he's stupid too and you're the only intelligent one within a ten-mile radius, aren't you? Stop acting so superior, Zoe. Can't you just be a normal girl for once? Come on, do it for me. Be just a little bit stupid, so I won't feel inferior.'

Leda took Zoe by the arm and pulled her back to the classroom. Roberto was sitting at his desk, brooding. He was looking out of the window, like someone who was pretending nothing had happened, but you could tell that he was agitated. He was fidgeting in his seat and tapping his pen on the desk. Zoe glanced over at him and smiled to herself (just inside, not so that anyone would notice). She thought how silly the whole thing was. It was like one of those American shows for teenagers, set in schools with lockers and gyms and proms. You knew that they were stupid, but if you started watching them you couldn't tear yourself away. What on earth was going to happen next? Tune in to find out.

Zoe was in no particular hurry to find out what was going to happen next in her own little soap opera. They had English next lesson and their teacher had promised to read them a great story. She was so good at reading stories and making characters come to life that everyone loved it when she read to them. As always, she launched straight into the story, without telling them what it was. It felt like being gently led into another dimension, leaving the normal world behind, with its desks and whiteboard and familiar faces. Zoe sighed and relaxed and allowed herself to be swept away.

'Hi, Roz. How are you doing?' asked Zoe on the phone that evening.

'Fine. That's what you're supposed to say when someone asks you that, isn't it?' Roz replied, sounding gloomy.

'But I really want to know how you are.'

'In that case, I guess the answer will have to be: I don't know.'

'Is it Paul?'

'Oh, Paul's busy with his own stuff, as always. And I'm busy with his stuff too. Trying to find out what his stuff is, I mean. You know, running around after him to see what he's up to.'

'And what does he think about that?' Zoe asked.

'Oh, he enjoys it. He likes everyone to adore him. And they usually do. He's such a good musician that everyone just rolls over for him. Never mind if in reality he's a selfish pig who always gets whatever he wants.'

'But if you know that he's like that . . .'

'It's love, my dear Zoe. Don't they say love's blind? Well, it's not true. Love can see perfectly well, but it chooses not to notice if it sees something it doesn't like. So, as far as I'm concerned, Paul is wonderful and that's that.'

'Maybe you should spend more time with other boys . . .'

'I can't,' sighed Roz. 'Don't you understand? My friends are all at music school. We study together, we have band practice together, we perform together . . . We do everything together. Everything revolves around the music and my sax.'

'And you love your sax, don't you?'

'Yeah, absolutely. Playing the sax is the only thing that makes me feel good. And it's also the only thing I like doing on my own. Anything else, I have to be surrounded by people. And there are always lots of people around Paul. Even if he's not there, the others talk about him all the time. What a mess, eh? Anyway, how are you doing? I'm sorry. I just keep talking about myself. How are things with Roberto? He seems really nice.'

'Yes, but he's acting all jealous at the moment. He thought I was interested in an older boy. How stupid can you get?'

'Well, maybe he's stupid because he's so young. If you ask me, he's too young for you. Girls are always more mature. We want a bit more than boys our age have to offer. They're just big kids really. Don't you think?'

'I'm not sure.'

'So, what's this older boy like?'

'He's nice. And cute.'

'And do you like him?' Roz asked.

'I've never looked at him like that. I mean, I didn't think he even knew I existed until the day before yesterday.'

'You think? You're so blind that I bet he's had his eye on you for months and he's been trying to attract your attention, and you didn't even notice.'

'I don't think so,' replied Zoe carefully.

'Whatever. Let me know how it turns out.'

'Hey, do you want to come out with us on Saturday afternoon?' Zoe said.

'Going out on Saturday afternoons is for babies. We all meet up on Saturday evening at someone's house. We listen to music and chill out. Quite a lot of people smoke. I don't. It's bad for your throat, so I can't, because of my sax. And it's pretty disgusting too. Anyway, got to go, Zoe. See you.'

After Roz's hurried goodbye, Zoe stood there in the corridor, looking down at the phone in her hand and feeling a bit foolish. Was she really blind, like Roz said? Or was it Roz who had a twisted idea of reality? Roz seemed so unhappy. It was just as well she had her music. But would that be enough for her?

Zoe wouldn't know what to do with herself if she didn't dance. That thought kept popping into her head as she thought about Roz and the notes of liquid gold that she made with her sax. Perhaps because when you were dancing that was all you thought about. It was as though all of your troubles (the complications of friendship, the difficulties of love, if you could call it love) were pushed into a corner, or carefully folded away, like bulky blankets that you folded up and squashed down so that they'd take up less space. The space had to be all about your moving body and the mind that was making it move, with no distractions from anywhere else.

Zoe put the phone down and glided to her room in two short and elegant leaps. She didn't usually dance outside school, but this evening she wanted to dance. She freed herself from her jeans, which were quite loose fitting, but still felt like a layer of cardboard. Then she took her T-shirt off, and her socks, until she was standing there in her vest and pants. With bare feet, in the limited space of her room, she improvised a very short dance – a sequence of familiar steps, the kind that you can do with the minimum of effort, because you've spent so many years studying them.

She didn't really know how Roberto (silly, silly Roberto) felt when he tried to be a choreographer, but she could imagine: it must be wonderful to invent a story made up of steps and gestures. She couldn't do it herself. *We're all different.* Roberto was jealous. How silly of him. She wasn't jealous. Zoe hadn't even been jealous when

Alissa told her that she once thought she was in love with Roberto. We don't all feel the same things. A step, another step. A turn. We can't all be the same and we have to learn to take other people as they are. A step, a turn. You need to do a lot of turns when you're dancing in a small space. You had to learn to accept them. A step. To accept Roz without getting angry with her, because there was no point, because she needed to get things off her chest, because maybe it was only by talking about it that she'd slowly come to understand that Paul's music was the best thing about him, and that Paul was not the music, even if he was the one who made it. To accept Roberto's silly demands, which were like the temper tantrums of a little boy who wanted a toy all to himself. But she needed to make him understand that she wasn't a toy. To accept Leda and all of her silliness, which was never meant to hurt anyone – she was just a bit daft and sometimes a little dangerous. To accept others and to accept herself as she was.

I don't play a musical instrument and I'm no good at choreography. But I am a ballerina. That's what I am. A ballerina.

CHAPTER ELEVEN

A Film or Two

Roberto kept himself to himself for the next couple of days. Zoe just let him get on with it. She tried not to look in his direction or to spy on him and she made an effort to act as though nothing had happened. She did quite a good job too, because she was certain that she'd done nothing wrong and that Roberto was behaving like an idiot. Anyway, she had so many other things to think about, what with rehearsals for the recital, tests and dance lessons. Now that the novelty of the pointe shoes was over, they were back to focusing on their technique: serious, solid, predictable.

She felt just as calm, and also curious, when Roberto came up to her on the stairs on Friday afternoon and stopped just in front of her, so she had to stop too. All he said was, 'I've got a present for you.'

Zoe smiled to herself. Did he really think he could make it all better with a present? Then she thought she'd take a look at the present first and then decide. Roberto slipped a flat parcel into her hands, wrapped in shiny paper with blue patterns on it. From the shape and weight of it, it looked like it might be a DVD. Then Roberto surprised her, because instead of staying there and waiting while she unwrapped the present, or suggesting that they should watch it together, he just gave her a little wave and ran down the stairs without looking back, as though he didn't even want to see how she reacted to the present.

Zoe decided to delay the pleasure of opening the present and take her time over it. So she didn't open it at school, but waited until she got home. She went home alone, without waiting for anyone. She wanted to think about all the things that had happened in recent days, about Roberto, Leda, Roz, Alex . . . And then, in her room, she found out what the present was – a film called *The Company* by Robert Altman. It was about a dance company, and Zoe hadn't seen it before. Roberto knew she hadn't seen it, because they – or rather, he – had talked about the film a few weeks earlier.

Unusually, peace reigned in the house that evening. Mum and Maria were out at Maria's gym class, Sara was goodness knows where with her friends, and it was too early for Dad to be home. So, with all of the sofa to herself, Zoe settled down to watch the film.

At one point in the film there was an open-air performance in a park in Chicago. The audience sat in front of a stage that looked like a black shell, lit by two rows of white globes running all the way around the seating area. A couple of young dancers danced a beautiful *pas de deux*. A pianist and a cello player played the live accompaniment and, as is often the case with cello music, it had a rather melancholy, wistful feel. The dancers were clearly performing a love story. The female dancer was wearing a short blue dress and dancing barefoot. You could see the weather was really bad. The wind was blowing and the people in the audience were wearing coats and scarves. Before long, flashes of lightning lit up the audience and the rain was pouring down. By the end of the dance, the audience were sitting under umbrellas, but no one left, because they were all so entranced by the dancers. The audience was just a sea of coloured umbrellas, twitching and bobbing about in the wind, but everyone sat there, watching the *pas de deux* as though the calmest of moons were hanging in the sky. Of course, the dance was a huge success and the audience shot to their feet to applaud at the end, with and without umbrellas. Then afterwards, it was all congratulations and flowers in the ballerina's dressing room, and dinners and parties, but there were also scenes of the ballerina at home by herself, crying and taking care of her injured feet.

Sara came home while Zoe was watching the film. Very quietly, she slipped off her shoes and curled up on the sofa next to Zoe and they watched the dance scene together. It was a beautiful scene and full of things that were left unsaid.

When the film was over, Zoe put the DVD back in the box and Sara said, 'It's a nice film, but it's all so dreadfully serious, isn't it? I think I preferred *Billy Elliot*. You know, that scene where he was really, really happy. I can't remember why, but he started dancing and he danced right out of the house and through the village without stopping, like he'd gone crazy, doing all those weird jumps and things. That was a sad film in parts, but it's the really happy bit that I remember. And then he gets into ballet school and he's in *Swan Lake* at the end and it's a happy ending. This film's not like that. It's all so serious. It makes it look as though ballerinas have a really hard time of it and that they're sad a lot of the time. Oh, and then the poor girl gets injured, so someone else dances her part. Wouldn't that be heartbreaking!'

'But *Billy Elliot* is all about the beginning of the

story,' said Zoe. 'He has to work really hard to be accepted as a ballet dancer and that's what the film's all about. We don't see what happens next at ballet school once he finally gets in. We just know that by the end of the film he's a great dancer. This film shows you what a dancer's everyday life is like. You know, it's really amazing, because they're part of this great dance company, but there's a lot of routine stuff too. That's what can be really exhausting. But the most wonderful, special moments are when you go on stage and have to perform.'

'I think you like this film more because you identify with the ballerina. You know, she actually looked a bit like you. Her eyes and hair were a bit darker than yours, but there is a certain resemblance.'

If only that were true, thought Zoe. Sara was just being nice. She did like the way the ballerina was so passionate and hardworking and melancholy though. She also enjoyed the film because it was an honest account of what happens in a dance company. It didn't matter that it didn't really have a happy ending. That was fine.

Roberto had given her a good present. She picked up the cordless phone and took it to her bedroom so that she could call him. 'Thank you. I really enjoyed the film,' she said.

'Oh, good,' he replied. 'I was sure that you'd like it.'

'Yeah, it was great. My sister Sara prefers *Billy Elliot* though,' Zoe said. 'Did you know they've turned it into a musical?'

'Yes, but they say it's really hard to get tickets. Mum read in the paper that the good seats are sold out months in advance, but we should definitely try and get hold of a couple of tickets some time.'

'Mmm, absolutely. And thanks again for the DVD. I think I might watch it again this weekend,' Zoe said. 'See you at school, Roberto.'

'Oh,' Roberto said, and Zoe could hear the disappointment in his voice, because he knew that she'd deliberately mentioned the weekend and said she'd see him at school because she didn't want to spend time with him that weekend.

'Okay,' he said. 'See you on Monday.'

Maybe by Monday, Zoe thought, as she went to put the cordless phone back in its cradle, everything would be all right again. Maybe her anger would have dissolved by then. No matter how nice a present was, it wasn't enough to make everything better all by itself. You had to really believe it inside as well. She might bump into Alex in the corridor, and say hi and ask him what he was doing in the end-of-year recital, and he would tell her, quite calmly, the way friends do. She'd ask him if he'd seen *The Company*, and of course he would have seen it and he'd have something intelligent to say, something for her to think about. Leda might be waiting in ambush around a corner, ready to draw her own conclusions, but Zoe couldn't care less. She would make her own way forward, hurrying a little, because the end of the year always had such a frantic feeling to it, partly because of the desire to finish things off and go on holiday, but also because of the wish to enjoy every single moment of everything that was going on – the excitement of the recital, that *Billy Elliot* kind of mad happiness mixed with relief and satisfaction; and the tension of the exams, which made you feel so alive somehow. Exams were certainly scary, because you didn't know how things were going to turn out, but it felt good to make an effort, to make things happen. It was so much better than just letting things happen to you. *Yes,* thought Zoe, *you have to make things happen.*

CHAPTER TWELVE

Surprises

Leda and Lucas were holding hands. It was such an amazing sight that Zoe couldn't pretend she hadn't noticed. When she saw them standing there at the front door, waiting for her, hand in hand, she just stared at them. 'What are you two doing? Are you crazy?'

'No,' Leda answered with a huge grin, hanging on to Lucas's arm. 'We're happy.'

Lucas actually looked embarrassed, rather than happy. You could tell by the way he was shifting his weight from one foot to the other, and it wasn't even the start of one of those Scottish dances that their teacher Kai liked so much, and which he danced and taught with such enthusiasm. Zoe had the feeling that if Lucas let his feet have their way, they'd run off and escape, but she wasn't quite sure why. If what Leda said was true and they *were* happy, why did Lucas look as though he'd rather be somewhere else entirely, like on a planet in another galaxy, for instance?

Zoe didn't have the opportunity to question Leda and find out how she'd managed to persuade Lucas (or 'won his heart', as she'd no doubt say) and what exactly had happened and when. They made their way to the park, where they found Roberto, who was already sitting on the back of their usual bench. So much for not seeing him until Monday! He waved at them to come over and join him.

'Weren't we supposed to be going shopping for a new T-shirt for you?' Leda said to Lucas.

'Oh, why don't we just stay here? It's not as though I don't have anything to wear,' he answered. He freed himself from Leda's clutches and went over to Roberto with obvious relief.

'Lucas is right,' Roberto said. 'It's such a nice day. Why would we want to hide away in the shops? It's always complete chaos in town on Saturday.'

It's chaos here too, Zoe felt like saying. Everywhere was a complete chaos on Saturday afternoon. Babies in pushchairs, toddlers on tricycles, children on bikes, half-naked joggers, and that funny group of foreign women who always met at the same bench every Saturday, and then started singing sad, faraway songs in an unfamiliar language.

It was a nice day though. The sun was warm on her bare arms, and Roberto was looking at her with a mixture of suspicion and anxiety, as though he was waiting for something to happen. Was she still angry? Yes, she was a bit. Did he understand why? There was no way to find out while the others were there.

Leda was staring dreamily at Lucas and Lucas seemed kind of happy, but kind of agitated, like a cat on hot bricks. What about Zoe? How did she feel? She felt calm but perhaps a little empty – it must have been the effect of all that sun pouring down on her head and heating her up and making her feel very light-headed, like a balloon that was about to fly away. Now that she thought about it, it would be nice to fly away, to rise up above the grass and the flowers and the trees and the fountain and the buildings and look at everything from a height, like when you're on a plane that's just taken off and you suddenly see the shape of things that you can't grasp from close up – the roads, the houses, the city. But maybe she didn't want to understand anything right now. She felt fine and that was enough. It was almost summer, and then her mind and body could go on holiday. Yes, she had the end-of-year recital and the exams to do, but she'd coped with them before and she'd cope with them again. She might not feel entirely calm, she might be a little nervous, but she'd get through them. They were nice things to do, as well as achievements to be gained – milestones on the way to growing up. Zoe got up off the bench and ran over to the fountain. She ran differently today – she was a little more relaxed than usual, letting the wind run its fingers through her hair, with her head back and her face warm in the sun.

'Where are you off to? Have you gone bonkers?' Roberto called after her, his voice far, far away in the distance. Zoe was all alone in that moment. She dropped down on to the edge of the fountain and plunged her hand into the water, right up to her wrist. The cold water made her cry out and took her breath away. Wasn't the world a wonderful place to be? Wait for it, wait for it. Here comes another sharp, clear insight. Yet another thought for *The Ballerina's Handbook*:

I think I've been a little too serious up until this point. To be a ballerina, you need to be cheerful, bright, full of light and life. You have to want to challenge yourself, to have adventures. To be brave. To be strong. Not to mention a little mad, because feeling all of those emotions at once really can send you quite crazy.

That was how Zoe felt right then. A little crazy, wonderfully crazy, and so very alive. What a great way to start the summer!

BEATRICE MASINI

Have you read them all?

Book 1 – Dance Steps
Another term at Ballet Academy brings even tougher challenges for Zoe and her friends. Leda is growing too tall and Laila is making everyone miserable. And then there's the end of term show to put on . . .

Book 2 – A Question of Character
As Zoe begins character dance classes, life seems to become more eventful – Leda is turning frosty, but Roberto seems friendlier than ever!

Book 3 – Friends Old and New
With Madame Olenska away, a new teacher brings a new style of teaching to the Academy – how will everyone react? Lucas is also offered the chance of a lifetime and the reason for Alissa's absence is discovered.

Coming Soon:

Ballet Academy

BEATRICE MASINI

Book 5
Dancing in Milan

Zoe's over the moon – she's been chosen to take part in a dance course in Italy! There's only one problem – Laila is going too and when they are together, sparks usually fly . . .

It will also give Zoe a chance to meet Roberto's family who live in Milan, and spend some time with him, but she and Roberto haven't been getting on very well lately so will this be a good or bad thing?

Book 6
A Tutu Too Many

A new student, Donna, joins the Ballet Academy, and is staying with Zoe and her family. It's not long before Zoe is feeling stifled, feeling that she has someone watching her all the time and has to involve Donna in everything she does.

As if that weren't enough, Madame Olenska is growing unhappy with the whole class, sparking off all kinds of doubts for the young ballerinas . . .

BEATRICE MASINI

The World of Ballet

Step into the wonderful world of ballet!
This beautifully illustrated book is filled with
everything you love about ballet – all the steps and
jumps, the stunning costumes, the best-loved ballets
and your favourite ballet stars are revealed by
Zoe and her Ballet Academy friends.

Discover behind-the-scenes secrets and find out
everything you ever wanted to know about the elegant,
graceful, amazing world of ballet!

Ballet Academy

Join in at:

⭐ ⭐

www.balletacademy.co.uk

⭐ ⭐

Discover more about:
⭐ the books
⭐ the dancing
⭐ the Academy
⭐ and lots more!